Marshall County Public Library
@ Hardin

Phoebe was still *in*
his arms, gazing *up,* *trying*
to make sense of *a* *man*
holding her.

This man sitting beside Sunny.

They were sitting at the end of the pew, in case Phoebe decided to roar and they had to take her out.

Anyone looking at her and at Max might think...

Don't go there, Sunny thought, *this is a fantasy.* There'd never been time or space for her to think of a love life.

She gazed down at her hands, at the lines and calluses formed by years of hard work, at the absence of rings. She stretched them out and suddenly, astonishingly, Max's fingers were closing over hers.

"Good hands," he said in a low voice. "Honorable hands."

She should... She didn't know what she should do. Had he known what she was thinking? How many hands had this man seen that looked like hers? None.

She should tug her hand back and the contact would be over. That was the sensible course, the only course, but she couldn't quite manage it. His grasp was warm and strong. Good.

Fantasy enveloped her again for a moment, insidious in its sweetness. To keep sitting here, to feel the peace of this moment, this place, this man...

Ingram
DEC 2 7 2017

Marshall County Public Library
@ Hardin
Hardin, Ky 42048

Dear Reader,

Last year a new warehouse opened right where I walk my dog. A Christmas warehouse! My family was horrified because they knew me, and their suspicions were justified. Two weeks before Christmas, a giant white swan with a glittering red-and-gold bow tie appeared in our front window for all the passing fishermen to admire, and for my husband to cringe at every time he saw it. But he grinned as well, because...well, Christmas is that time of the year. I go overboard with the emotion as well as the glitter.

Which brings me to *The Billionaire's Christmas Baby*. My title pretty much explains my idea—to write a story around a billionaire, Christmas and a baby. Wow, there's a dream package. Someone would need to be special to deserve all three.

And Sunny is special. The story opens to find her hard at work, scrubbing hotel floors to earn enough money to fund her family's Christmas. She has no time for nonsense. No time for billionaires?

But there's always time for billionaires, especially at Christmas, so Sunny needs to share. Thus, I've gift wrapped Max with his adorable baby and handed them to you. In lieu of glittering swans. Enjoy.

Marion

The Billionaire's Christmas Baby

—

Marion Lennox

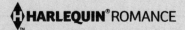

If you purchased this book without a cover you should be aware
that this book is stolen property. It was reported as "unsold and
destroyed" to the publisher, and neither the author nor the
publisher has received any payment for this "stripped book."

Recycling programs
for this product may
not exist in your area.

ISBN-13: 978-0-373-74462-6

The Billionaire's Christmas Baby

First North American Publication 2017

Copyright © 2017 by Marion Lennox

All rights reserved. Except for use in any review, the reproduction or
utilization of this work in whole or in part in any form by any electronic,
mechanical or other means, now known or hereinafter invented, including
xerography, photocopying and recording, or in any information storage
or retrieval system, is forbidden without the written permission of the
publisher, Harlequin Enterprises Limited, 225 Duncan Mill Road,
Don Mills, Ontario M3B 3K9, Canada.

This is a work of fiction. Names, characters, places and incidents are
either the product of the author's imagination or are used fictitiously,
and any resemblance to actual persons, living or dead, business
establishments, events or locales is entirely coincidental.

This edition published by arrangement with Harlequin Books S.A.

For questions and comments about the quality of this book,
please contact us at CustomerService@Harlequin.com.

® and TM are trademarks of Harlequin Enterprises Limited or its
corporate affiliates. Trademarks indicated with ® are registered in the
United States Patent and Trademark Office, the Canadian Intellectual
Property Office and in other countries.

Printed in U.S.A.

Marion Lennox has written more than a hundred romances and is published in over a hundred countries and thirty languages. Her multiple awards include the prestigious RITA® Award (twice), and the *RT Book Reviews* Career Achievement Award for "a body of work which makes us laugh and teaches us about love." Marion adores her family, her kayak, her dog and lying on the beach with a book someone else has written. Heaven!

Books by Marion Lennox

Harlequin Romance

The Logan Twins

Nine Months to Change His Life

Sparks Fly with the Billionaire
Christmas at the Castle
Christmas Where They Belong
The Earl's Convenient Wife
His Cinderella Heiress
Stepping into the Prince's World
Stranded with the Secret Billionaire

Visit the Author Profile page
at Harlequin.com for more titles.

**Praise for
Marion Lennox**

"The story is one of a kind and very interesting.
Once I started, I couldn't stop."
—*Goodreads* on *Stranded with the Secret Billionaire*

CHAPTER ONE

SHE'D FORGOTTEN GRAN'S cherry liqueur chocolates.
No!

Sunny Raye abandoned her scrubbing and gave in to the horror of her memory lapse. The discount store near home brought in mountains of chocolates for Christmas. They were cheap and delicious, but they'd be sold out by now.

It was ten at night and she was bone-weary. She'd agreed to work overtime because she needed the pay—Christmas was expensive—but all she wanted now was her bed. Tomorrow was Christmas Eve and she was rostered to work again from eight to five. Where could she find time to buy Gran's chocolates, and how much would she need to spend?

Aaagh!

'How long does it take to scrub one floor?'
Uh-oh.

The stain on the tiles was hard against the bathroom door. She hadn't been able to shut it, which meant she was in full view of the guest sitting at the desk. He was annoyed? The feeling was mutual. This was a job for Maintenance, not for a scrubbing brush.

But Sunny's job was to make the guest feel that

this was a scrubbed stain rather than a missed-by-Housekeeping stain. *Keep him happy at all costs*—that had been the order. When Max Grayland was in town the hotel fell over itself to make sure all was right with his world. Heads would roll over this stain, but it wouldn't be her head.

Enough. She dried the floor with care, then rose. Oh, her knees hurt, but perky must be maintained.

'I'm so sorry, sir,' she told him brightly, as if this was the start of her shift rather than two hours after she was supposed to be gone. 'It appears to be a bleach stain, possibly from hair dye. It should have been noticed and I apologise that it wasn't. I can arrange for the tile to be replaced now, if you like.'

Ross in Maintenance would kill her, but she had to offer.

'However, it'll involve noise and you may wish us to leave it until morning,' she added. 'Meanwhile, I can assure you it's clean and totally hygienic.'

'Leave it then.' Max Grayland pushed the documents he'd been working on aside and rose, and she sensed he was almost as weary as she was. With reason? She knew he'd flown in from New York this morning, but Max Grayland crossed the globe at will. Surely travelling in first class luxury prevented jet lag?

How would she know? Sunny had never flown in her life.

But he did look tired. Rumpled.

He was a financial whiz, she'd been told, a man in his mid-thirties, at the top of his game. The media described him as a legal eagle, and that was what he looked like. He was tall, dark and imposing, with deep, hooded eyes and a body that seemed toned to the point of impossible.

He was still wearing the clothes he'd worn at check-in but he'd ditched his jacket, unbuttoned the top of his shirt and rolled his sleeves. His after-five shadow looked like after five from the night before.

What was a man like this doing looking exhausted? Didn't he have minions to jump to his every whim?

He stalked over and stared at the stain as if it personally offended him, but she had a feeling he was seeing far more than the stain. He raked his dark hair and his look of exhaustion deepened.

'Leave it,' he growled again. 'Thanks for your help.'

That was something at least. Most of the guests who stayed in the penthouse didn't bother to say thank you.

'I'm sorry I can't do more.' She edged past him, which was a bit problematic. She was carrying a mop and bucket and she had to edge sideways. She didn't edge far enough and her body brushed his.

She smelled the faint scent of aftershave, something incredibly masculine, nice…

Sexy.

Good one, Sunny, she thought. This morning her hair had been tied into a neat knot, but the knot had loosened hours ago and she hadn't had time to redo it. After a day's hard physical work in the hotel's often overheated rooms, her curls were limp and plastered against her face. Her uniform was stained. She knew she smelled of cleaning products—and she was suddenly acutely aware that the guy she was brushing past was a hunk.

A billionaire hunk.

Get a grip.

'Goodnight, sir,' she said primly and headed for the door. For some reason she wanted to scuttle. What was he doing, unsettling her like this?

Cherry liqueur chocolates, she told herself firmly. *Focus on imperatives.*

But a rap at the door made her pause.

Her training told her to melt into the background, which was impossible when she was in his room, carrying an armload of cleaning gear.

'What the…?' Behind her, Max Grayland growled his displeasure. 'I don't need anyone else fussing over this. Tell your people to leave it.'

He was assuming it'd be the manager, coming to grovel his apologies. She hadn't reported that she couldn't fix the stain, though. Brent wouldn't be here yet.

But access to the penthouse suite floor was security locked. Stray visitors didn't make it up here.

'You're not expecting anyone, sir?'

'I'm not,' he snapped. 'Tell them to go away.' And he retreated behind his desk.

There was nothing for it. She put down her mop and bucket, pushed her stray curls back behind her ears—*gee, that'd make a difference*—and opened the door.

And almost fainted.

She knew the woman in front of her. Of course she did—this was a face that was emblazoned on billboards, on buses, on perfume advertisements nationwide. Exotic and glamorous, Isabelle Steinway's pouty face was her fortune. She was famous for…well, for being famous. Her fame had just started to fade when news of her pregnancy had hit the tabloids, and for the last few months the media had been going nuts. There'd been gossip galore, fed by Isabelle's publicity machine—a secret father, the body beautiful doing all the 'right things' and selling those 'right things' as exclusives…

And then nothing. For the last few weeks Isabelle had inexplicably gone to ground. There'd been a publicity statement that she wished for privacy for the birth, which was a huge ask for the public to believe.

But she was here now, glamorous as ever, in a

tight-fitting frock that made a mockery of the fact that she must have just given birth.

A night porter was standing behind her, looking anxious. Nigel must have been badgered into allowing her up here, Sunny thought, but who could blame him? The media reported that what Isabelle wanted, Isabelle got, and one pimply-faced teenage porter wouldn't be enough to stand in her way. Nigel looked terrified. And deeply unhappy.

He was pushing a pram and the pram was wailing.

But Isabelle was ignoring the pram. The moment Sunny opened the door, she swept in, brushing her aside as if she was nothing. As indeed she should be. She should disappear, but Nigel was blocking her way. He'd pushed the pram into the doorway, stopping her leaving, and his gaze was that of a rabbit caught in headlights.

They were both stuck.

She might as well turn and watch the tableau in front of her.

The penthouse had been decorated for Christmas. A massive tree sparkled behind them. There were tasteful bud lights hanging from the windows, and through those windows the lights of Sydney Harbour glittered like a fairy tale.

The two centrepieces in this tableau were also like something out of a fairy tale. Yes, Max looked exhausted, but this man would look good after a week in the bush fighting to survive. The warrior image suited him—business clothes seemed almost inappropriate.

And Isabelle? She was wearing a silver-sequined frock that would have cost Sunny a year's wages or more. How had she got into it so soon after giving birth? There must be a whalebone corset somewhere under there, Sunny thought. Her blonde hair was shoulder-length, every curl exquisitely positioned. Her crimson mouth was painted into a heart shape. Everything about her seemed perfect.

Except the pram behind her. The wail coming from its depths was growing increasingly desperate.

But Isabelle seemed oblivious to the wail. She was focusing on Max, her glower designed to skewer at twenty paces.

'She's yours,' she spat and Sunny watched Max react with blank incredulity.

'I beg your pardon?'

'Do you think I want her?' Isabelle's voice was vituperative. 'I never wanted her in the first place. Your father... "Have a baby and I'll marry you," he said. "You'll be taken care of for life. You'll never have to work again."' Her voice was a mock imitation, a vicious recount of words obviously said long ago. 'And now...your father's will... Yeah, he changed it, like he promised he would. His whole fortune for this kid, held in trust by me until the age of twenty-one. But he never said anything to me about a son! I would have aborted. No, I'd have never got pregnant in the first place. So now he's dead and the will says everything goes to his youngest son. But there's only one son, and that's you. You get it all, and my lawyer says I'll even have to file a claim for this one's maintenance. Do you think I slept with a seventy-eight-year-old egomaniac and carried his kid for maintenance?'

Her voice ended on a screech. She sounded out of control, Sunny thought—there was real suffering under there. Real betrayal.

She looked again at Max and saw blank amazement.

'I have no idea what you're talking about,' he managed.

'So welcome to the real world,' Isabelle snapped, fighting to get her voice back to a reasonable level—which was tricky seeing she was talking over a baby's screams. 'She was born last week. Two days after your father's heart attack. You can do a paternity test if you like—I don't care. She's your father's. Her papers are with her. Everything's in the pram. Her name's Phoebe because Phoebe's the midwife who delivered her and when I said I didn't care she sounded shocked so I said I'd call her after her. But now…if you think I'll sit at your father's funeral like a grieving widow you have another think coming. My lawyers will be contacting you for compensation.'

'Isabelle…' Max sounded gobsmacked. 'I'm so sorry…'

'I don't want your sympathy,' Isabelle hissed. 'Your father lied through his teeth to persuade me to have this kid and I might have known… But it's over. There's a house party up north starting tomorrow, with people who really matter. I have no intention of taking that…' she gestured at the howling pram '…with me. You inherited everything your father possessed, so she's yours.'

'You're planning to abandon your baby?' Max's voice was filled with shock, but also the beginnings of anger. 'Yours and my father's baby?'

'Of course I'm abandoning it. It was a business contract and he broke it.'

'So he planned a son—why? To keep me from inheriting?'

'If he'd told me that I might have even done something,' Isabelle snapped. 'For the amount of money he promised me, I could have fixed it. Sex selection's illegal in this country but he had enough money to pay for me to go abroad. But the stupid old fool didn't even have the sense to be upfront.'

'You know he had a brain tumour. He died of a heart attack but he had cancer. You know he wasn't thinking straight.'

'I don't know anything and I care less,' Isabelle snapped. 'All I know is that I'm leaving. My lawyers will be in touch.' She whirled back to the door, blocked now by the goggling Nigel and the pram. 'Get out of my way.'

Nigel, shocked beyond belief, edged the pram aside so Isabelle could shove her way past. She stalked the four steps to the elevator and hit the button.

The elevator slid open as if it had been waiting.

'Isabelle!' Max strode forward, but the terrified Nigel had swung the pram back into the doorway and bolted, straight through the fire door.

The pram held Max back for precious moments.

The elevator doors slid closed and the fire door slammed.

Isabelle and Nigel were gone.

CHAPTER TWO

THE FIRE DOOR looked very, very appealing.

Cleaning staff were supposed to be invisible.

'Enter discreetly. If guests are present, act as if you're a shadow. Listen to nothing and if there's the slightest sense of unease disappear and go back later. If there's a problem call Housekeeping and have a guest relations manager handle it.'

That had been the mantra drilled into her two years ago when she'd taken this job and Sunny liked it that way. There was too much drama and worry in her personal life to want any more at work.

So, like Nigel, she should bolt for the fire door. Except that would mean pushing past Max, pushing past the pram, possibly even dripping her mop on both.

He'd have to move. He'd have to tug the pram inside, so she could edge out.

Meanwhile, she tried melting against the wall, acting like part of the plaster, hoping he wouldn't notice her.

Though there was a sneaky little voice that was thinking, *Whoa, did I really see what I just saw? Where was a camera when she needed it? The media would go nuts over what had just happened.*

Right. And she'd lose her job and she wouldn't get one again in the service industry and what else was she trained for? She'd left school at fifteen and there'd only been sporadic attendance before then. She was fit for nothing except blending into the wall, which she'd done before and she had every intention of doing now.

Max didn't seem to notice her. Why would he? He'd just been handed a bombshell.

He walked cautiously forward and peered into the pram. The wails increased to the point of desperation and the look on Max's face matched exactly.

She expected him to back away in alarm. Instead he leaned over and scooped a white bundle into his arms. The wails didn't cease. He stood, looking down into the crumpled face of a newborn, and something in his own face twisted.

The pram was still blocking her path but with the baby out of it she could pull it to one side. She could leave.

She edged forward and Max turned as if he suddenly realised he had company.

'You…'

She was still standing with her mop and bucket. Her cleaner's uniform was damp down the front. Her curls were escaping from her regulation knot. She looked nothing like the image of immaculate efficiency the hotel insisted she maintain. Brent would have kittens if he could see her now, she thought, but there was nothing she could do about it.

'Yes, sir.'

'Do you know anything about babies?'

There was a loaded question. The answer was more than she wanted to think about, but she wasn't going there.

'If you need help, you might ring Housekeeping,' she suggested, clutching her mop and bucket like a shield and lance. 'Or I can ask them to send someone up.' She listened to the wails and softened just a little. 'She sounds like she needs feeding,' she suggested. 'You might check the pram for formula, or Housekeeping could provide some. Goodnight, sir...' And she edged forward.

She didn't make it two steps. He was in front of her, blocking her way.

'You're not going anywhere,' he growled. 'Take her.'

'I'm the cleaner.' She wasn't putting her mop and bucket down for the world.

'Until I find someone else, you're here to help. You stay until I get Housekeeping up here. Put that gear down and take her.'

'Sir, she's your baby...'

'*She is not my baby.*'

It was a deep, guttural snap that shocked them both. It appeared to shock even the baby. There was a moment's stunned silence while all of them, baby included, took a breath and reloaded.

Max recovered first. Maybe he had the most to lose. He strode to the door, slammed it shut, pushed the pram in front of it and then walked straight to her. He held the bundle out, pressing it against her.

She could hold her mop and bucket with all the dignity she could muster, or she could take this bundle of misery, a crumpled newborn.

Did she have a choice? *What's new?* she thought bitterly. *When there's a mess, hand it to Sunny.*

She set the cleaning aids aside and took the bundle. As if on cue, it—she—started wailing again.

'I'll ring Housekeeping,' Max snapped. 'Stop her crying.'

Stop her crying. Right. In what universe did this man live? A universe where babies had off switches?

But as he stalked to the phone she relented and peered into the pram.

There was a bag tucked in the side. She investigated with hope.

A folder with documents. A tin of formula. A couple of bottles. Two diapers.

Okay, this baby's mother wasn't completely heartless. Or…she was pretty heartless, but Sunny had coped with worse.

She sighed and headed for the penthouse's kitchenette. She'd seen Max make himself a hot drink a few minutes ago. Blessedly, he'd overfilled the kettle, so she had boiled water. She balanced

Marshall County Public Librar @ Hardin
Hardin, Ky 42048

baby in one hand, scoop and bottle in the other, made it up, then ran cold water in the sink to immerse the base of the bottle to cool it.

The wailing continued but she could hear Max in the background on the phone. 'What do you mean, no one? I want a babysitter. Now. Find someone. An outside agency. I don't care. Just do it.'

A babysitter at ten o'clock, the night before Christmas Eve? Christmas was on a Sunday this year, which meant today was Friday. The whole world—except the likes of hotel cleaners—would have started Christmas holidays today. Celebrations would be almost universal and every babysitting service would be stretched to the limit.

Good luck, she thought drily, but then she looked down into the baby's face. Phoebe was tiny, her face creased in distress, her rosebud mouth working frantically. How long since she'd been fed?

This little one's mother had handed her over without a backward glance. This man didn't want her.

There were echoes of Sunny's background all over the place here, and she didn't like it one bit.

She needed to leave.

She could feel sogginess under her hand. And the baby…smelled?

'Get someone up here. Get me the manager.' Max was barking into the phone, but she tuned it out. How long since this little one had been changed?

A tentative examination made her shudder. *Ugh.* She gave up on the thought of a simple change and headed for the bathroom. She stripped off all the baby's clothes, then used the washbasin to clean her. The wailing was starting to sound exhausted, but the baby had enough strength to flail her legs in objection to the warm water.

But Sunny was an old hand. Washing was brisk and efficient. She had a replacement nappy but no change of clothes. No matter—she was warmed and dry. Sunny wrapped her expertly in one of the hotel's fluffy towels, carried her back to the living room, checked the bottle, settled down on the settee—had she ever sat on anything so luxurious in her life?—and popped one teat into one desperate mouth.

Then finally the world settled. The silence was almost overwhelming.

Even Sunny was tempted to smile.

Such little things. A clean bottom. A feed. *Deal with the basics and worry about tomorrow tomorrow.* That had been Sunny's mantra all her life and it served her still.

But now she had time to think.

Next on her list was getting out of here.

She glanced across at Max, still barking orders into the phone. He looked like a man at the peak of his powers, a business magnate accustomed to ordering minions at will. He was trying to summon minions now.

But there weren't many Australian minions who'd drop everything at this hour to be at his beck and call.

It's not my problem, she told herself and turned her attention back to the bundle in her arms.

She was a real newborn. A week old at most, Sunny thought, suddenly remembering Tom. Sunny had been nine years old when Tom was born. She remembered weeks where she couldn't go to school, where she'd struggled with a colicky newborn, where she'd felt more trapped than she ever wanted to feel again.

But she wasn't trapped now. This little one had a family and that family wasn't her. What was she—half-sister to the man on the phone? She even looked like him, Sunny thought. Same dark hair. Same skin tone—she looked as if she'd spent some of her time in utero under a sun lamp.

Did she have the same nose? It was difficult to say, she decided. It was a cute nose.

She was a cute baby. Wrapped in her white towel, she looked very new, and totally defenceless. She was still sucking her bottle but desperation had faded and tiredness was starting to take over. Sunny could feel the little body relax, drifting towards sleep.

Great. She could pop her back into the pram and leave.

'She's going to sleep?'

The deep voice, the hand on her shoulder made her start with shock. She hadn't heard him leave the desk and walk over to her.

He was standing behind her, staring down at the baby.

'She was well overdue for a feed,' she managed. Why had he put his hand on her shoulder? To hold her down? To keep her here?

Or maybe he simply wanted contact, reassurance that he wasn't alone.

He was alone, she thought. She was leaving.

'Can I ask you to keep quiet about what's happened?' he asked.

'Sorry?' Her mind had been heading in all sorts of directions, one of them being the way she was reacting to this man's touch. How inappropriate was that? Somehow she managed to focus.

'I work on the staff here,' she managed. 'I signed a confidentiality agreement.'

'And you'll keep it? The media will pay for a story like this. If they make you an offer... I'll meet it.'

'I said I signed a confidentiality agreement,' she retorted, flushing. 'You think I'd break it for money?'

'I have no idea what you'd do.' He lifted a corner of the towel so he could see her name, embroidered discreetly under the hotel logo on her uniform. 'Sunny Raye. What sort of name is that?'

'Mine.' She was starting to feel a bit glowery.

'I'm sorry. I didn't mean to be personal.'

'That's good. There's no need to be personal. I'm a cleaner and I need to go back to work.'

The bottle was finished and laid aside. Phoebe's eyes were closed. Her tiny rosebud mouth was still making involuntary twitches, as if the bottle was still there.

She was beautiful, Sunny thought, but then she'd always been a sucker for a baby. A sucker for being needed?

Of course. Wasn't that the story of her whole life?

'I'll pop her back in the pram,' she suggested. She wanted to rise but the hand was still on her shoulder. The grip tightened.

Uh-oh. It *was* pressure.

'You can't leave.'

Watch me, she thought. And then she thought of the discreet little disc attached at her waist, like an extra button on her uniform. A security disc.

Even at exclusive hotels—and this was surely the most exclusive in Sydney—incidents happened. Guests drank too much. They were away from home. The normal rules often didn't seem to apply.

Female staff were taught how to back away fast from situations, but as a last resort there was the disc. Three pushes and she'd have security guards here in moments.

Protecting her from this man?

He wasn't harassing her for himself, though. He needed her for his baby.

Right, and she had chocolate cherry liqueurs to find and sleep to have and gifts to wrap before she returned here for her Christmas Eve shift tomorrow. *Harden up, girl*, she told herself. *Even use the security disc if you must. You're a cleaner. This is not your business.*

She rose, despite the pressure of his hand. He released her—with real reluctance, it seemed—and stood back.

'She's fed and changed, sir,' she told him, facing him head-on. 'I'll pop her back into the pram if you like, but I need to go. Though…' A sudden pang of conscience made her add, 'I'll clean the bathroom before I go.'

'You just cleaned the bathroom.'

'Yes, sir,' she said woodenly and he frowned and opened the bathroom door. And recoiled.

'My giddy aunt…'

'Yes, sir,' she said primly. She used his distraction to slip her sleeping bundle back in the pram. The pram was a mess too, filled with forms, baby clutter, a stupid elephant mobile strung across the top. But this wasn't her concern either. She pulled out the loose stuff and laid it on the floor. Already his swish suite was starting to look as if a bomb had hit it, but this guy should have a few hours' peace to sort things out. 'Would you like me to clean?' she asked primly.

'Of course.'

'There will be a charge,' she said. 'The stain on the tiles was our responsibility, but extra cleaning for normal hotel use incurs an out-of-hours service fee.'

'You're charging me for cleaning?' He sounded incredulous.

'I'm sorry, sir.' She glanced at her watch. She'd been here for almost an hour and it'd go on the hotel's time sheets. If she wanted to be paid for overtime, she had to report it. And he had to pay.

'That's unreasonable.'

She was overtired. She was at the end of a stupidly long shift. She'd had enough.

'Unreasonable for me to be paid for scrubbing? Really?' So much for being a shadow. She let her glower have full sway. 'I know, I'm just a money-hungry grub.' Grub was the truth. She felt filthy. 'But your decision shouldn't be my business. I've done what I was sent to do, and more. Ring Housekeeping if you want the bathroom cleaned, and discuss charges with them. My shift is finished.' And she took a deep breath and strode to the door, prepared to depart with as much dignity as she could muster.

She swung the door open, and Brent was there.

Brent. Assistant hotel manager. Guy on the way up. Obviously here to appease.

He looked at her and grub didn't begin to describe the look he gave her. Okay, she was filthy. She'd been down on her knees scrubbing. She'd just tended one distressed baby. The wet splotches on her uniform—*you try bathing a baby in a bathroom sink*—could have been anything. Maybe they were 'anything'. Maybe she smelled as well. Who knew? Who cared? She was over this.

'What seems to be the problem, Miss Raye?' Brent said, silky-smooth, and she thought, *I am in so much trouble.* Cleaning staff should never, ever be noticed, much less by the assistant manager of the entire hotel.

'Sir, I was sent up to clean a stain in Mr Grayland's bathroom.' She hauled back on her temper, doing her best to make herself sound subservient. Yes, she'd let her anger hold sway for a moment but she needed this job. She needed to retreat fast. 'I've done my best with the tiles but the stain needs Maintenance. I was about to report it, but before I could leave Mr Grayland requested urgent assistance with his baby.'

'It's not my baby!'

She ignored the savage growl from behind. She was too busy salvaging her career to care.

'I'll talk to you later,' Brent told her, in the tone used the world over to convey menace to underlings when on the surface all had to be rosy. 'Wait for me before you leave.' And he turned to Max and put on his full managerial, ingratiating smile. 'Now, sir...'

She was free. She'd have to wait in the change room for Brent to tell her what he thought of her but at least she was out of here. She grabbed her trusty mop and bucket and headed for the fire stairs. No elevator was going to be fast enough.

'Stop her.'

'Sir?' Brent sounded confused. Sunny had almost reached the stairs. Almost gone...

'If you're here to tell me there's no babysitting service available, I want this woman to stay,' Max snapped. 'And I'm prepared to pay whatever it takes to keep her.'

Brent hadn't got where he was by being thick. Or slow. He'd got it in one. Her desperation to leave. Max's desperation to have her stay. Without seeming to move, Brent was suddenly, seamlessly between Sunny and her precious stairwell.

Yikes.

'Put your equipment down,' he told her and once again she got that look of disdain. Brent was immaculate, smoothly urbane, doing what the guest needed. That he had to put himself so close to an actual cleaner was obviously distasteful in the extreme—that he had to talk to her was worse.

But he was blocking her path and he was making it clear she had no option. She put her mop and bucket down again but she wasn't buying into whatever was happening. She put her hands behind her back, looked at the floor and waited. A good little cleaning lady…

'Sir…' With Sunny trapped, Brent turned back to Max. 'We apologise but there is no babysitting service available. If you'd booked your baby in earlier…'

'I didn't have a baby earlier,' Max snapped. 'And I told you before—she's not my baby.'

'She's his sister,' Sunny muttered because she'd just spent twenty minutes cleaning and feeding a little girl and it suddenly seemed important—no, imperative—that someone laid claim to her. But as she said it, memories surfaced.

A social worker, taking Chloe from her arms. *'You can't take care of her, sweetheart.'*

And Sunny yelling back with all the might of her small self. *'But she's my sister!'*

Those memories weren't appropriate now, but they were strong enough to make her lift her gaze to Max and look defiant. But his anger blazed back at her.

'I asked you to keep quiet about what's just happened,' he snapped.

Right. She went back to staring at the floor, but not before she'd seen the stab of shock as she'd said the word *sister*. Not before she'd seen him glance back at the pram with a look that was suddenly uncertain.

Up until now his reaction had been one of shock

and anger. Something had messed with his world and he needed to put it right. But now…his face suddenly showed a new emotion.

Sister…

What sort of family did this man have? Obviously there'd been friction between father and son. Where was the rest of his family?

Why did the word *sister* register with such shock?

But Brent was forging on, trying to make sense of what was happening. Focusing on the near target.

'Mr Grayland had to ask you to be quiet?' he demanded.

'He's talking of my confidentiality agreement,' she told him, still staring at the floor. 'He doesn't wish me to talk of what's happened outside this room.'

'Or inside either,' Max snapped and amazingly Brent came to her defence.

'Miss Raye is required to report anything that happens in this hotel to me. But of course the confidentiality agreement extends to me as well. I'd like Miss Raye to leave. She has work to be getting on with, and as a cleaner she can hardly be of any use to you.'

'But you don't have a babysitter for me.'

'No, sir.'

'And Miss Raye knows how to care for babies.' Brent sent her an uncertain glance. He wasn't sure where to go with this. 'Is this true, Miss Raye?'

'Please…' She needed to get out of here. She spoke directly to her boss. 'I'm at the end of a double shift. If you'll excuse me…'

'But you do know about babies?'

Did she know about babies? It was practically the only thing she did know. But now wasn't the time for hollow laughter. *Be invisible. Disappear.*

'She does,' Max said, suddenly softening. 'She washed her and fed her.'

'Miss Raye?' Brent reacted with shock. 'That's not in your list of duties. Our insurance doesn't cover…'

'Damn your insurance.' Max's anger flared again, but once again he turned to Sunny. Who was still desperately looking at the floor. 'Miss Raye, you obviously know how to care for a baby. She's sleeping now. You're at the end of a double shift? You must be tired.' He gazed around the suite and she could almost see cogs whirring. 'This living room has a massive settee. Your manager… Mr…' He looked in query at Brent.

'Cottee,' Brent told him smoothly. 'Brent Cottee.'

'Thank you. Mr Cottee can no doubt send up nightwear, toothbrush, anything you need to stay the night. My bedroom has an en suite bathroom so you can be separate. Mr Cottee, I'm prepared to pay full babysitting services for the night, doubled, plus the same amount to Miss Raye personally.' He looked uncertainly back at the pram but forged on, plan in place. 'This could suit.'

'Suit who?' Sunny muttered.

'Suit me,' Max said smoothly. This obviously wasn't a man who let objections trouble his path. 'I can't believe money wouldn't be useful at this time of the year.'

Was he kidding? Of course it would. It'd be glorious.

And the alternative? By the time she got home it'd be midnight and she was due to start work again at eight. Gran and Pa wouldn't even realise she hadn't come home.

'The insurance…' Brent bleated but it was a weak bleat. He looked almost hopeful.

'I'll sign a waiver,' Max told him. 'Miss Raye might not have childcare credentials but I've seen enough to know I want her.'

'You're on duty again tomorrow?' Brent demanded.

'Yes, sir, at eight.'

He nodded. 'Then it seems satisfactory.' The fact that she'd just done a double shift, that she could well be up all night with a newborn and she had to work tomorrow seemed to worry neither of them. But then she thought…double money. A double shift today, payment for a double shift tonight and then tomorrow's shift… She could almost pay for Tom's tooth to be capped with that. Tom was working all summer to pay his uni fees but the money wouldn't stretch to dentistry.

And baby Phoebe was asleep. With luck, it'd be just a couple of quick feeds during the night.

So… She had her back to the wall but she also had Max Grayland at her mercy.

She could try.

So she tilted her chin and met his gaze square-on.

'I agree,' she told him. 'On one more condition.'

'Which is?'

'I need the biggest, fanciest box of cherry liqueur chocolates that money can buy, gift-wrapped and delivered here before I leave work tomorrow. If you can find me those, we have a deal.'

'You're kidding,' Max said, astounded.

'Miss Raye…' A hissed warning from Brent.

But she ignored him. Tomorrow night would be crazy. Christmas Eve would be in full swing before she got home. She'd have cooking, gift-wrapping, hugging, greeting, chaos… And Gran was expecting her chocolates.

'That or nothing,' she told him and Max met her look. A muscle twitched at the side of his mouth. For a moment she even saw a twinkle. Laughter?

'They're that important?'

'That or nothing,' she repeated and the twitch turned into a smile.

It transformed his face. She'd thought he seemed harsh, autocratic, bleak, but suddenly he was laughing at her…no, with her, she thought, because his smile seemed almost kind. His gaze was still on hers, holding her, blocking out the rest of the world.

Oh, my… It was enough to take a girl's breath away.

Actually, it had taken her breath away. She needed to find herself a nice, quiet place and remember how to get it back.

But Max had moved on. He turned to Brent. 'Mr Cottee? Cherry liqueur chocolates?'

'I'm sure Miss Raye doesn't mean it,' Brent said.

Sunny opened her mouth to retort but she didn't need to. Max got in before her.

'Miss Raye doesn't have to explain,' Max said smoothly. 'It's me who requires it. The biggest, fanciest box of cherry liqueur chocolates money can buy, delivered to this suite before Miss Raye finishes work tomorrow.'

At least this was easy. This hotel seemingly had links to every service industry in town. The cost would be high but Brent knew enough not to quibble. 'Yes, sir. We can do that.'

'And a qualified child carer to take over from Miss Raye in the morning.'

'Yes, sir,' Brent said and maybe Max heard the uncertainty in Brent's voice or maybe he didn't. Sunny did, but she wasn't saying anything. Tomorrow's worries were for Max, not for her.

'Then that's settled,' Max said smoothly. He glanced at his watch. 'I have a conference call coming in from New York in five minutes. I'll work from my bedroom. Miss Raye, you can use the separate bathroom out here, the kitchenette and anything you need from room service. Mr Cottee will no doubt organise it. I'll see you in the morning.'

So that was it. A child, dumped...

No.

'Say goodnight to her,' she managed.

'What?'

'You heard. Say goodnight to your sister.'

'She's asleep.'

'Yes, and you're family. Who knows what she can hear or not hear, but it seems to me you're all the family she's got. Say goodnight to her.'

'Miss Raye...' Brent sounded outraged but she was past caring. Once again she met Max's gaze full-on, defiant, and memories were all around.

Her childish voice from the past. *She's your baby. You should feed her...* And her mother slapping her hard and slamming the door as she left.

This man wasn't in a position to slap her. She could still walk away. This was her only chance—

maybe baby Phoebe's only chance—to find herself someone who cared.

And once again something twisted on Max Grayland's face. He gave her a look she didn't understand, then wheeled and walked back to the pram.

'Goodnight,' he muttered.

'Properly,' she hissed. 'Touch her. Say it properly.'

'Miss Raye!' Brent was practically exploding but she wasn't backing down.

'Do it.'

And Max sent her a look that was almost afraid. There was a long silence. He knew what she was demanding, she thought, and he was afraid of it.

But finally he turned back to the pram. He gazed down for a long moment at the sleeping baby—a newborn, who was his half-sister.

And his expression changed yet again. He put a finger down and stroked the tiny face, a feather touch, a blessing.

'Goodnight,' he said again and then looked back at Sunny. 'Satisfied?'

'That'll do for now,' she said smugly and smiled.

The look he sent her was pure bafflement. But then his phone rang. He snagged it from his pocket, glanced at the screen and swore. 'My conference call…'

'We'll take care of everything, sir,' Brent said smoothly. 'Take your call. Goodnight.'

'Thank you,' he said formally and, with a last uncertain glance at Sunny, he turned, walked into his grand bedroom and closed the door behind him.

CHAPTER THREE

WHAT HAD WOKEN HIM? Probably nothing, he conceded. His body was still on New York time, even if in reality his body was lying in a king-sized bed in a suite overlooking Sydney Harbour.

Four a.m.

Today was the day he'd bury his father.

Nothing less important than this would have dragged him half a world from New York for Christmas. His usual method of coping with the festive season was to have his housekeeper fill his apartment with food, set himself up with the company's financial statements and use the break to conduct an overall assessment. It was a satisfying process, even if it meant a nasty shock for the occasional employee returning to work in the New Year.

But now… His mobile laptop didn't allow him to access the innermost secrets of the Grayland Corporation. Too risky. He'd brought some work but it wouldn't take all his concentration—and he needed his concentration to be taken.

His father's funeral…

And a baby sister?

What had the old man been thinking?

He knew his father's illness had made him con-

fused over the last year. There'd never been any
love lost between them at the best of times, but
Colin Grayland had been proud of his company
and fiercely patriarchal. There'd never been any
hint that he'd disinherit Max, but that had been
mainly through lack of choice, and for the last
twelve months the old man had been obsessively
secretive.

Max had learned of Isabelle's existence two
days ago. As sole heir, the lawyers had transferred
his father's personal banking details to him before
he'd left New York. A quick perusal had shown
a massive payment to Isabelle almost a year ago.
Then another seven months back—was that when
Isabelle had her pregnancy confirmed?—and then
regular deposits until the last few days of the old
man's life.

He'd assumed Isabelle had been his father's
mistress but the amounts had been staggering,
and now he knew why.

Colin Grayland had paid for a baby. A son, if
Isabelle was to be believed, though he must have
been too confused to think of the ramifications,
or the possibility, of a daughter.

And now he was landed with a baby. His sister?

The thought was doing his head in. He had no
idea how to face it.

Lawyers? Surely it was illegal to dump a baby.
Isabelle would have to take the baby back.

But she didn't want her.

So adoption? For a baby who was…his sister?

He couldn't think straight. He needed a drink, badly.

Was he kidding? It was four in the morning.

Yeah, but it was midday in New York. He travelled often and his rule for coping with jet lag was not to convert to local time unless he was staying for more than a few days. So his body was telling him he'd stayed up late and now he'd overslept. It was thus time for lunch and a man could have a whisky with lunch.

He wouldn't mind a sandwich either. Room service was his go-to option in such circumstances but he couldn't wake the pair in the next room.

He didn't want to think about the pair in the next room.

But the next room also held the minibar. A packet of crisps and a whisky would set him up to sit and write the final version of what he had to say at his father's funeral.

He definitely needed a whisky to write what had to be said.

If you can't say anything nice, don't say anything at all. That had been a mantra drummed into him by some long ago nanny, and it normally held true, but a huge section of Australia's business community would turn out. They'd be expecting praise for a man who'd made his money sucking the resources of a country dry.

He did need a whisky, but that'd involved the minibar. Which involved walking into the next room.

They were in the next room. Sleeping.

Or…had something woken him? Maybe they were awake and he was wasting time, hanging out for a snack. Besides, he was paying her.

Do it.

The minibar was by the door through to the elevators. Moonlight from the open drapes showed the way.

He moved soundlessly across the room.

And stopped.

A sliver of moonlight was casting a beam of light across the settee.

The woman—Sunny Raye, her name tag had said—was sleeping. The settee had been made up as a bed, loaded with the hotel's luxury sheets and duvet and pillows.

They weren't being appreciated.

The pillows were on the floor. The duvet had been discarded as well, so her bedding consisted of an under-sheet and an open weave cotton blanket pulled to her waist.

Having discarded the pillows, she was using her arm to support her head. That'd give her a crick neck or a stiff shoulder in the morning, he thought, but he was distracted.

She was wearing an oversized golfing T-shirt with the hotel's logo emblazoned on the chest. Her curls, caught up in a knot when he'd last seen her, were now splayed over the white sheet. Brown with a hint of copper. Shoulder-length. Tangled.

Nice.

Earlier he'd thought she was in her thirties. Her face had worn the look he often saw on hotel staff at the lower end of the pay scale—pale from not enough sunlight, weary, worn from hard physical work.

Now, though, he revised his age guess downward. She looked younger, peaceful in sleep, even vulnerable?

And then a faint stir in the crook of her arm had him focusing to her far side.

The baby was asleep beside her.

In what universe…? Even he knew this!

'What do you think you're doing?' The exclamation was out before he could stop himself. She jerked awake, staring up, as if unsure where she was, what she was doing, what he was.

She looked terrified.

He took a couple of fast steps back to give her space. He didn't apologise, though. He might have scared her but he was paying for childcare. He wanted childcare—not a baby suffocated in sleep.

'She shouldn't be sleeping with you,' he said, louder than he should because there were suddenly emotions everywhere. He shouldn't care. Or should he care? Of course he should because this baby was his sister, but that was something he didn't have head space to think about. The idea, though, made him angrier. 'I know little about babies but even I know it's dangerous to sleep in the same bed,' he snapped. 'Surely you know it too.'

He saw the confusion of sleep disappear, incredulity take its place. She pushed herself up on her elbow, making a futile effort to push her tumbling curls from her eyes. The baby slept on beside her, neatly swaddled, lying on her back, eyes blissfully closed.

'You want an apology?' she demanded and an anger that matched his was in her voice. 'It's not going to happen. I'm a cleaner, not a nanny.'

'I'm paying you to care for her.'

'Which I'm doing to the best of my ability. Sack me if you don't like it. Look after your baby yourself.'

'I might have to if you won't.'

And the anger in her face turned to full scale fury. All traces of sleep were gone. 'Might?' she demanded. '*Might?* How much danger would she have to be in before you showed you care enough to do that?' She rose to face him. She was wearing T-shirt and knickers but nothing else. Her legs were long and thin and her bare feet on the plush carpet made her seem strangely vulnerable. His impression of her age did another descent. 'You want me to leave?'

'I want you to do what you're being paid for.'

'Believe it or not, I am.' She glared her fury. 'Your sister's sleeping on a firm settee that has no cracks in the cushioning and a sloping back that's too firm to smother her. See the lovely soft settee cushions? They're over there. See my pillows and my nice fluffy duvet? They're over there too. So I'm sleeping on a rock-hard settee with no cushions and no duvet.'

'Because…'

'Because the moron who set up Phoebe's pram filled it with a feather mattress, which is far more dangerous to a newborn than how I've arranged things. The mattress is stuck in the pram. Did you notice? Of course not. But I did when I checked her before I went to sleep. Some idiot's screwed in an elephant mobile—for a newborn!—and they've caught the fabric of the mattress. I'd need to rip the mattress to get it out and feathers would go everywhere and you'd probably make me pay for it. Housekeeping's up to their ears in work and it would've taken them an hour to get me a cot, even if there was one available, which I doubt. I didn't fancy putting her to sleep on the floor and by the time I'd figured all that out I was tired and over it so she slept with me. She's been as safe as I could make her. But take over, by all means. I've a crick in my arm like you wouldn't believe. It's been over four hours since she fed so she's likely to wake up any minute but she has formula and the instructions are on the tin. Forget the money. I couldn't give a toss. I'm leaving.'

There was a stunned silence. He stared at the settee, bereft of anything soft. He looked at the still miraculously sleeping Phoebe.

He looked at the furious, tired, overworked woman in front of him and he felt a sweep of shame.

He was way out of his comfort zone and he knew enough to realise he had to back off.

'I apologise.'

'Of course you do. You've given me a lecture. Now you're expecting to go back to your nice comfy bed and leave me holding the baby. I don't think so.' She was a ball of fury, standing in her bare feet in the near-dark, venting her fury. Righteous fury.

'I could double the chocolates,' he said, feeling helpless.

'You think you can buy me with chocolates?'

'I thought I already had.'

'Get stuffed,' she told him and flicked on the table lamp and started searching among the discarded bedding for her uniform.

And, as if on cue, the baby woke.

Phoebe. His sister.

She didn't cry but he was attuned to her, and the moment her eyes flickered open he noticed.

She was so tiny. So fragile. She was swaddled in a soft wrap, all white. Her hair was black. Her eyes were dark too.

She looked nothing like Isabelle.

She was all his father.

She was all...him?

Dear heaven...

'The formula's on the sink,' Sunny said, sulkily now, as if she thought she was misbehaving. 'Make sure the bottle's clean and the water's been boiled.'

'I can't.'

'You don't know what you can do until you have to. Believe me, I know.' She snagged her uniform from the floor and headed for the bathroom. 'She's all yours.'

And, as if the idea terrified her, Phoebe opened her mouth and started to wail.

'Well,' Sunny said, over her shoulder. 'Pick her up.'

'I can't.'

'Don't be ridiculous.' She reached the bathroom and closed the door firmly behind her.

Help...

The baby's wails escalated, from sad bleats to a full-throated roar in seconds. How could such a beautiful, perfect wee thing turn into an angry, red-faced ball of desperation?

Was it the thought of being left with him? He knew nothing of babies. Zip.

This was his sister. Half-sister, he reminded himself, but it didn't help.

The bathroom door was still firmly closed.

Somehow he'd sacked his babysitter for no reason.

How could he have thought she'd been unsafe? Sunny had her as safe as she could make her. She'd checked her before she'd gone to sleep. She'd noticed the too-soft mattress.

He hadn't.

Tentatively he lifted the wailing bundle into his arms. Even the movement seemed to soothe her, and her sobs eased. Did she sense then how close she was to being abandoned?

The bathroom door opened again. Sunny stood there, still rumpled by sleep, but back in her stained uniform, her sensible shoes, her workday gear.

'Where will you go?' he asked, because he couldn't think of anything else to say.

'Home.'

'Where's home?'

'Out west. Because there's no public transport at four a.m. it's an hour's bike ride but that's none of your business. I have no idea why I'm telling you.'

'Stay.'

'In your dreams.'

'Sunny, I'm sorry,' he said and he was. Deeply sorry. He looked at her tilted chin, her weary pride, her humiliation, and he felt a shame so deep it threatened to overwhelm him. That she was tired and overworked he had no doubt. Hotel cleaners were a race apart from the likes of him. They were shadows in the background of his world.

This one was suddenly front and centre.

And then he had a thought. A bad one.

'You know about babies.' The words were suddenly hard to form. 'Are you…? Do you…?'

She got it before he could find the words. 'You mean do I have my own baby strapped to my bike, waiting for me to finish my shift? Or left in a kitchen drawer with a bottle of formula laced with gin?' She gave a snort of mirthless laughter. 'Hardly. But I've raised four, or maybe I should say I've been there for them while they raised themselves. They're grown up now, almost independent, apart from Tom's teeth. But that's my problem and you have your own. Goodnight and good luck.' She headed for the door.

But he was before her, striding forward with a speed born of desperation. Putting his body between her and the door. But her words were still hanging in the air even as he prevented her leaving.

Four? He thought of how old she was, and how young she must have started, and he thought of a world that was as removed from his as another planet.

And she got that too. She gave a sardonic grin. 'Yep, I started mothering when I was five, with four babies by the time I was nine. Life got busy for a while, and I admit I even co-slept. Not just with one baby—sometimes all five of us were in the same bed. But, hey, they're all healthy and your Phoebe's still alive so maybe I'm not such a failure. Now, if you'd let me leave…'

He didn't understand but now wasn't the time to ask questions. 'Please,' he said, doing his best to sound humble. 'Stay.'

'You can cope.'

'I probably can,' he admitted. 'If you refuse then I'll pay for a taxi to take you home and to bring you back tomorrow.' He hesitated. 'But, to be honest, it's Phoebe who needs you. She shouldn't be left with someone so inept.'

She hesitated, obviously torn between sense and pride. It was four in the morning. Even in a taxi it'd take time for her to get home, he thought. She was weary and she had to be back here again in a few hours.

Logic should win, but he could also sense something else, an anger that didn't stem from what had just happened.

He was replaying things she'd said. *'How much danger would she have to be in before you showed you care?'* She thought he didn't care and she was right. He had nothing invested in this baby. Tomorrow he'd see lawyers, come to some arrangement, pay whatever it took to reunite her with her mother.

Except…she looked like him. And this woman was looking at him with judgement.

'I'll do it on one condition,' she said.

'I've already said more chocolates. And I'll double your pay.'

'Gran's got the appetite of a bird. One box is fine, and I'm not taking any more of your money.'

'Then what?'

'I'll stay on condition you change her and feed her now,' she told him. 'I'll watch but you do it.'

'I need to write the eulogy for my father's funeral.' He said it harshly but he couldn't hide the note of panic. 'That's why I'm awake.'

'Oh, that's hard,' she said, her voice softening. 'I'm sorry about your dad.' But then her chin tilted again. 'But your dad's dead and this little one's not, and it seems to me that someone's got to go into bat for her. So you change her and feed her and then you can do what you like. I'll go back to caring. My way. But it's that or nothing, Mr Grayland.'

She met his gaze full-on, anger still brimming. She was flushed, indignant, defiant, and suddenly he thought… *She's beautiful*.

Which was an entirely inappropriate thing to think and, as if she agreed with him, baby Phoebe opened her mouth and wailed again.

'Fine,' he said helplessly. 'Show me how.'

'It'd be my pleasure,' she said and grinned and went to fetch a diaper.

* * *

She could have insisted that he take the baby back to his bedroom to feed her, but Max's tension was tangible. She could almost reach out and touch it. According to the media, this man was one of the most powerful businessmen in the world, but right now he was simply a guy who'd been thrust a baby he didn't know what to do with.

And didn't she know what that felt like?

So she helped prepare the bottle, showed him the skin test for heat and agreed there should be some scientific way—there probably was but who had time to search for a thermometer at four in the morning? She watched as he did the diaper change, blessing herself that she'd asked the hotel shop to send up extras. It took him three tries to get it right without messing with the adhesive tapes.

Then she retreated to her settee and gave herself the luxury of leaning on pillows, while Max sat at the desk by the window and fed his little sister.

When she'd fed her last time it had been a desperate feed, a baby over-tired and over-hungry, relieved beyond measure that here was the milk she needed. She'd sucked with desperation.

This time, though, things had settled. Phoebe was warm and dry, and the bottle was being offered almost as soon as she'd let the world know she needed it. She seemed content to suck lazily, gazing upward at the world, at the man who was holding her.

They hadn't turned on the main light. Sunny was watching by moonlight, seeing the tension slowly evaporate as Max realised he was doing things right. As Phoebe realised things were okay in her world.

It wouldn't always be as easy as this, Sunny thought. What did this man have in store for him? Colic? Inexplicable crying jags? Teething? All the complications that went with babies. Would he cope with them?

Of course he wouldn't. The thought was laughable. He'd been so desperate for help that he'd employed her, a cleaner. He'd employ someone more suitable the moment he could.

Still, she had to cut him some slack. He'd come to Australia for his father's funeral. All the world knew that. Colin Grayland had been a colossus of the Australian mining scene. His son had taken over the less controversial part of a financial empire that was generations old. He must have kept his head down, because she knew little about him. He'd been an occasional guest in this hotel. There was always a buzz when he visited, but it was mostly among the female staff because a billionaire who looked so gorgeous…well, why wouldn't there be a buzz? And there was also a buzz because his visits usually coincided with his father storming into the hotel, usually shouting.

Here in Australia, Colin Grayland had seemed to court controversy. He'd ripped into open cut mining, overriding environmental protections, refusing to restore land after it had been sucked of anything of any value. He had such power, such resources, that even legal channels seemed powerless to stop him.

His son, however, seemed to disagree with much of what the old man had done. The media gossip of clashes between the two was legion.

'So what will you say about your father tomorrow?' she asked into the silence and thought, *Whoa, did I just ask that?* Cleaner asking tycoon what his eulogy would be? But the man had said he'd woken to write the eulogy. Maybe she could be helpful.

She tucked her arms around her knees, looked interested and prepared to be helpful.

'I don't know,' Max said shortly.

'You don't know.' Phoebe was steadily sucking. The near dark lent a weird kind of intimacy to the setting. It was like a pyjama party, Sunny thought. But different. She watched him for a while, his big hands cradling his little sister, the bottle being slowly but steadily sucked. Okay, not a pyjama party, she conceded. Like…like…

Like two parents. Like the dad taking his share.

What did she know of either? Pyjama parties? Not in her world. And parents sharing?

Ha.

But now wasn't the time for going there; indeed she hardly ever did. Now was the time to focus on the man before her and his immediate problems.

Actually, his immediate problem was sorted for now. But his dad… She'd read the newspapers. The funeral would be huge. Every cashed-up developer, every politician on the make, even the Honourables would be there, because even with the old man gone the Grayland influence was huge.

And this man was doing the eulogy. In less than seven hours.

'I'd be so scared I'd be running a mile,' she told him. 'But then public speaking's not my thing. Are you thinking you'll wing it?'

'What, decide what I'll say in front of the microphone?'

'The way you're going, you'll need to.'

'Says the woman who won't give me time to think, who won't feed my baby.'

My baby. They were loaded words. She saw his shock when he realised he'd said them. She saw his horror.

'Hey, I'm happy to help with the speech,' she told him hurriedly. 'How hard can it be?'

And she watched his face and saw…what? A determination to steer the conversation away from the baby he was holding? Because he couldn't face what he was feeling? 'To say my father and I didn't get on is an understatement,' he told her. 'Look how little I knew of his personal life.'

'Because?' She said it tentatively. She had no right to ask, and no need, but he didn't have to answer if he didn't want to, and something told her that he wanted to talk. About anything but the baby.

'My parents were pretty much absent all my life,' he told her. 'I was an only child, with nannies from the start. My parents divorced when I was two and went their separate ways. I lived with whoever's current partner didn't mind a kid and a nanny tagging along, or the nanny and I had separate quarters if it didn't suit. But I was raised to take over the financial empire. It was only when I developed a mind of my own—and a social conscience—that I saw my father often. Our meetings have never been pretty. Maybe I should have walked away but I've been given enough autonomy to realise I can eventually make a difference. As he's grown older and more frail I've been able to stop the worst of his excesses. But now…to give a eulogy…'

She heard his bleakness and something inside her twisted. She thought of her own childhood, itself bleak. But she'd always had her siblings. She'd always felt part of a family.

But this was a man in charge of his destiny, as well as the destiny of the thousands of people he employed. She refused to feel sorry for him.

'Hey, reality doesn't matter at funerals,' she told him. 'No one's there for a bare-all exposé.

You want my advice? Tell them a funny story to start with, a personal touch, like how he wouldn't buy you an ice cream when you were six because you hadn't saved up for it. There must have been something you can think of, something like that'll make them all laugh and put them onside with you. Then give his achievement spiel. Look him up on Mr Google. That'll list all his glories. Finally, choke up a little, say he'll be sadly missed and walk off. Job done.'

He sent her a curious look. 'You want to do it for me?'

'I would,' she told him agreeably. 'But I'm working tomorrow. Eleven o'clock will see you at the lectern, and I'll be scrubbing bathrooms.'

'You can't take the day off?'

'To give your father's eulogy? I don't think so.'

He smiled. She sensed it rather than saw it. Nice, she thought, and hugged her knees a bit more.

It really was weirdly intimate, sitting in the moonlight in her almost-PJs, talking to this... stranger.

'I'm guessing here,' he ventured, sounding cautious. 'But am I hearing the voice of experience? You've worked out a eulogy for someone you didn't like?'

That was enough to destroy any hint of intimacy. She hugged her knees a bit tighter, needing the comfort.

'I might have.'

'These kids you looked after…were they your brothers and sisters?'

'It's none of your business.'

'It's not,' he agreed. 'But you know a lot about me now. It's dark, we're both tired and this is a weird space. I wouldn't mind pretending I'm not alone in it.'

And she got it.

He was sitting in an impersonal hotel half a world away from where he lived. He was holding a baby he hadn't known existed and later that morning he'd have to stand in a vast cathedral and speak about a father it sounded as if he'd loathed.

He felt alone? He felt as if he needed some sort of reassurance that he wasn't the only one who'd ended up in a mess up to their neck?

After tomorrow she'd never see this man again. Why not give it to him?

'I gave my mother's eulogy when I was fourteen,' she said and she felt rather than saw the shock her words caused.

'At fourteen…'

'There was no one else. Mum died of an overdose after she'd alienated everyone. I never knew my father. She had me a couple of years after she'd run away from home, and then there was a gap. Who knows why? Maybe she was responsible enough to use birth control for a while, but it didn't last. The next four babies came in quick succession and for some reason she kept us. But *kept* is a loose description. We were raised…well, we weren't raised. We lurched from one crisis to the next. Finally she died. The social worker said we didn't need to go to the funeral, but they hadn't found Gran and Pa then, so there was only us. And they'd already split us up. Daisy and Sam had gone to one set of foster parents, Chloe and Tom to another. It's hard to find foster parents for a fourteen-year-old, so I was placed in a home for… troubled adolescents and I was going nuts, wanting to see them. So when the coroner released the body for burial I made a king-sized fuss and said we all had to be at the funeral. Our case worker said she had reservations but she arranged it anyway. Then I figured I had to say something the kids could remember.'

'You did?' he demanded, sounding awed.

'I did,' she said proudly. 'I made them laugh by telling them about Mum's awful cooking. I reminded them of the way she could never get her toenails perfect and the way she had funny names for all of us, even if sometimes she couldn't quite remember which one of us she was talking to. They were sort of sad stories but I made them smile. Then, when we came out, the social worker had organised morning tea. I still remember the sausage rolls! And then she sat us down, very serious, and told us they'd found Gran and Pa. Apparently, they hadn't even known we existed! Mum had robbed them blind when she was young and then, when she knew they had no more money, she cut off all contact. But they're just… wonderful. I can't tell you how wonderful. They had somewhere we could live and they loved us straight away. So then we all lived happily ever after. Isn't that nice? So it's worth thinking of something good, even if it kills you to say it.'

There was an appalled silence. It stretched on and on and she thought *uh-oh,* she shouldn't have said. Kid of a drug addict? It was a wonder he even let her near his baby.

But it seemed he wasn't thinking that. 'You make me feel ashamed,' he said at last.

'There's no need to feel ashamed,' she said with asperity. 'Unless you intend to let a fourteen-year-old girl beat you at the eulogy stakes. Let me have Phoebe. You can write your eulogy in peace.' She unhugged her knees and headed over to take the baby from him.

But he held on, just for a moment.

'Thank you,' he said simply.

'You're paying me.'

'Not enough for what you're doing tonight.'

'I don't think you realise how big a deal Gran's chocolates are,' she told him. 'For those alone I'd have written your eulogy for you. Now, off you go and write. The intro's easy. Lords, Ladies, distinguished guests, ladies and gentlemen…there's the thing half done.' And she scooped the now sleeping baby into her arms and backed away.

She needed to back away, she thought. The look on this man's face…

This was a night out of frame. The intimacy between them was something that couldn't be replicated and could never exist in the light of day.

She needed to back off fast, and she did. And he let her.

'I'll write in the bedroom,' he managed and she nodded.

'You came out for something? Or to check on me.'

'I came out for a whisky.'

'It won't help the jet lag. Or the eulogy.'

'I know that,' he told her. 'And I don't need it any more. You've given me all I need.'

'Really?'

'Really.'

She grinned. 'Hooray. Advice by Auntie Sunny. Off you go then like a good boy and get it done.'

'Yes, ma'am,' he said and cast her a look she didn't understand. A look full of questions she couldn't hope to answer.

He rose and left.

She settled Phoebe again with care, and told herself to sleep.

Sleep didn't come. For some reason the memory of that appalling time, her mother's dreadful funeral, was suddenly all around her.

She was thinking too of the grand funeral waiting for Max tomorrow, and she was thinking there were similarities.

She hugged Phoebe because she suddenly needed the comfort and she thought again of the man through the bedroom door. Who did he hug?

It wasn't any of her business, but the question stayed with her until finally sleep overcame her.

Who did Max Grayland hug?

And the answer came with certainty. It was an answer written in the harshness of his voice, in the strain in his eyes, in the way he held himself.

The answer was no one.

CHAPTER FOUR

AT SEVEN THE next morning a brisk knock signalled the arrival of a hotel maid bearing a pristine uniform for Sunny. Behind her was a dour woman in her fifties. 'I'm from the hotel's childcare,' she announced.

'Excellent.' Sunny had answered the door still in her T-shirt and knickers. Yes, there were bathrobes in the suite but they were in the bedroom, where Max was either asleep or still writing his eulogy. She motioned to the sleeping baby. 'She's all yours.'

'She slept on the settee?' the woman demanded, shocked.

'She slept safely.' The low growl behind her made Sunny jump. Max. 'Thanks to Miss Raye. But maybe you can organise a cot.'

'Certainly.' The woman looked at Sunny in incredulity. 'I gather this was an emergency arrangement. Most unsatisfactory. However, you can now return to your duties.'

'Thank you,' Sunny said simply and grabbed her new uniform and headed for the bathroom.

'Miss Raye?' Max said.

'Yes?' She was desperate to disappear. The maid, the babysitter and Max were all looking at her. She was wearing a T-shirt and knickers and nothing else. Her tangled curls were flying every which way. She needed Superman's telephone booth, she thought grimly, one that showered her, cleaned her teeth, fixed her hair into a decent knot and dressed her in an instant. But instead she was forced to turn and face Max—who was wearing one of the gorgeous hotel bathrobes.

She glowered. She couldn't help herself.

'What's wrong?' he asked, looking bemused.

'What do you think is wrong? I need your bathrobe.'

And the toe-rag grinned. Grinned! 'Now? Shall I take it off?'

Oh, for heaven's sake. She could only imagine what he was wearing underneath—or not. 'Don't be ridiculous. If you'll excuse me...'

'Sunny...'

'Yes?'

'Come back before you finish tonight and collect your chocolates.'

'Can you arrange for them to be delivered to the staff quarters?'

'I need to ensure they're satisfactory. So here?'

'Fine,' she said, goaded, desperate to be away.

'And Sunny?'

'Yes?' They were all looking at her. She felt like a bug under a microscope. Helpless.

'Thank you,' he said.

He smiled. Oh, he shouldn't do that. That smile...

'Think nothing of it,' she said, trying not to sound grumpy. And…breathless in the face of that smile.

'And Sunny?'

'Yes.'

'I mean it,' he said, and then, before she knew what he was about, before she could even guess what he intended, he crossed the room, he placed a finger under her chin, he tilted her chin—and he kissed her.

It was a feather kiss. A trace of a kiss. It hit her forehead, not her lips. There was no reason at all for it to take her breath away, for her to stand stock-still as if she'd been seared.

Already he'd stepped back. He put his hands on her arms as if to steady her—why would he think she needed steadying?—and he was back to smiling at her. Quizzically. Almost mockingly.

'Your work was above and beyond the call of duty,' he said, his tone softening. 'Where's the form I need to fill in to give this staff member five stars? Or more.'

'Miss Raye!' It was the babysitter, appalled. 'Get your uniform on. You know the rules about fraternising with the guests. This will be reported…'

'It will be reported,' Max said, his gaze not moving from Sunny's face. 'Like the dispatches from Waterloo. Victory with all honour. Service like no other. Thank you, Sunny.'

'I'll… I'll see you this afternoon,' she managed,

clutching her clean uniform as if it were armour. 'I… Will that be all, sir?'

'Thank you, yes.'

Excellent. Or was it? She had no idea.

But her time here was over and she fled.

Give his achievement spiel. Choke up a little, say he'll be sadly missed and walk off. Job done.

He followed Sunny's advice pretty much all the way, though he couldn't quite manage the choking up part.

But he got away with it. The post-funeral luncheon, organised by his father's ex-secretary, was truly sumptuous and as he moved among the assembled dignitaries he received approving nods and handshakes from all sides.

'Well done, boy. We look forward to seeing you move into your father's footsteps. Business as usual, hey?'

In your dreams, he thought, but now wasn't the time to say it. Half these people were about to get a rude shock when their cosy business deals were turned on their heads.

That should be giving him satisfaction. And the death of his father should be making him emotional too. It had, a little, when he'd stood in front of the congregation and thought of the things most men could say of their fathers. That they'd been loved. That they'd be remembered with affection.

It was hard to feel affection for someone he'd

known only through business dealings, who he knew had scorned his ideas—and who'd paid to have someone bear a child to supplant him as heir.

And that was where his attention was as he mingled with the crowd, as he responded as expected, as he murmured pleasantries.

He was thinking of a baby called Phoebe.

And a woman called Sunny?

Why Sunny? Sunny was surely irrelevant, a hotel cleaner hired for the night. From now on he'd have proper, qualified staff.

To look after a child he didn't want?

A child no one wanted?

She was already messing with his plans. He'd intended to be on tonight's plane, back to New York. But walking away from his...walking away was impossible, and there was no way he could get paperwork in place fast enough to take her with him.

Even if he wanted to.

Did he have a choice?

And then he was thinking of Sunny again, of her fierceness, her courage, her care.

Sunny would expect him to care.

'Well done, lad.' It was one of his father's cronies, a financier with a finger seemingly in every crooked pie in the land. He'd had a beer or six and now walked up and clapped Max on the shoulder. It was as much as Max could do not to flinch. 'We'll be seeing you in Australia most of the time now, I imagine. This is where you can make the most money. Your father saw it. Any advice I can give you, feel free to ask. You're staying on for Christmas, I expect?'

And there was only one answer to that. He didn't even know where Isabelle was and he was the executor of his father's estate. One baby was therefore his priority. He was stuck.

He needed help.

Once more he thought of Sunny, in her absurd nightwear, her tangle of curls, with her smudged dark eyes and that glimmer of defiance against the world.

She was a hotel cleaner. She had no qualifications to take care of a baby, even if he wanted her to.

He'd seen the hotel manager this morning and made it clear that not only did he need to extend his booking, he wanted paid professional childcare, possibly until New Year. By which time he'd have it sorted. Surely?

'Yes, sir, I'm staying for Christmas,' he managed and the man clapped his shoulder again and gave him a beery grin.

'Well, Merry Christmas,' he boomed. 'May Santa be good to you.'

Just like he always was, Max thought wryly, and moved on to the next polite inanity.

If she didn't really need the chocolates she wouldn't be here. But they were Gran's treat, treasured from time immemorial. Or from that first Christmas when, as a frightened, defensive fourteen-year-old, Gran and Pa had suddenly appeared, miraculously wanting to help. And love. She'd had no money but the guy at the local discount sweets shop had watched her looking at the gaudily wrapped boxes and told her if she was prepared to spend a few hours breaking down cardboard boxes out the back she could have the box of her choice.

Gran had opened them on Christmas morning and cried. 'I would have cried even if they weren't my favourite,' she'd sobbed. 'Oh, Sunny…'

That memory still caused her to blink back tears, and it had her heading up towards the penthouse suite for the last time. She'd ditched her uniform. She was back in her all-weather jeans and T-shirt. Her bike was waiting. Christmas was waiting.

She knocked on the door and hoped this could be fast. It was after five already. The kids would be arriving at Gran and Pa's before she got there and she had so much to do.

There were voices coming from inside, male voices, raised, polite but urgent.

'I'm sorry, sir, but some things are impossible.'

'You're telling me there's no babysitter in this entire country?'

'There may well be babysitters, but we can't find anyone. The lady who worked for you today has finished her shift and left the hotel. All the agencies are closed. Most have been closed from midday and won't open again until next Tuesday. None of our staff are prepared to take the extra shifts at this short notice, and who can blame them? They all have their Christmases organised.'

'You're saying I'm stuck in a hotel for the next two days with *this*?'

For *this* was screaming her head off again, and the word caught Sunny as nothing else could. There was a part of Sunny that wanted to turn and flee. But…*this*?

She knocked harder and then almost fell inside as the door was wrenched open.

'You,' Max snapped and his tone was close to one of loathing.

Sunny was used to anger in every shape and form. She'd learned the best way to deal with it was to retreat, to make yourself invisible, but if you couldn't do that then stand up to the toe-rag. She'd even kicked one of her mother's boyfriends once. She had a scar under her hairline to prove it but she didn't regret it one bit.

She faced him head-on. *This.* The word was still reverberating.

'I've come for my chocolates,' she said and his anger was put on hold as he realised who it was.

'I'm sorry. Of course.'

And she should butt out—but she couldn't. 'Don't apologise to me,' she snapped. 'Apologise to your sister. Calling her *this*…'

'You heard.'

'I imagine half the hotel heard.'

'Miss Raye!'

Finally she had time to take in the other person in the room. The hotel manager. The head honcho himself. This man had eyes in the back of his head. She was wearing her staff lanyard but even without it he'd have known her name. This man had the reputation of knowing what went on in the hotel before it happened. His voice now held reproof, quiet but chilling. 'What are you doing here?'

'I'm collecting something that's mine,' she muttered. She needed to calm down. She valued this job.

'I have it.' Max snagged a box from the sideboard—and what a box! It was enormous, exquisitely wrapped in gold, with crimson bows that must be worth what she usually paid for the whole box. He handed it over and managed a smile. 'I'm sorry. There was no reason to snap at you. I am indeed grateful.'

'And your sister's not *this*.'

'I beg your pardon.'

'Don't say sorry to me. She's Phoebe. Not *this*.'

'No,' he said, chastised. 'I beg her pardon too.'

'She sounds like she needs a feed.'

'She's just had one. I have no idea what to do.'

'Miss Raye…' It was the manager again, smooth as silk. 'I hear you did an emergency stint as babysitter last night.' His eyes were calmly assessing. She could almost see the cogs turning. How to keep this most valuable client happy? He turned again to Max. 'Sir, Miss Raye doesn't have child-care qualifications but she's cared for your sister already. If you found her satisfactory… Miss Raye, if we offered double pay rates, and Mr Grayland, if it's satisfactory to you… Miss Raye, would you be prepared to stay on over Christmas?'

Oh, for heaven's sake…

She stood, clutching her chocolates, staring at the men before her.

To miss Christmas… Who were they kidding?

'No,' she said blankly. 'My family's waiting.'

'You're not married, Miss Raye.' The manager was stating a fact, not asking a question.

And that took her breath away. How much did the manager know about her? She'd been vetted when she'd taken the job at this prestigious hotel but this was ridiculous.

'I can't see that makes any difference,' she said stiffly. 'I need to go.'

'But Mr Grayland's stranded in an unknown country, staying in a hotel for Christmas with a baby he didn't know existed until yesterday.' The manager's voice was urbane, persuasive, doing what he did best. 'You must see how hard that will be for him.'

'I imagine it will be,' she muttered and clung to her chocolates. And to her Christmas. 'But it's…'

'None of your business,' Max broke in. 'But if there's anything that could persuade you... I'll double what the hotel will pay you. Multiply it by ten if you like.'

Multiply by ten... There were dollar signs in neon flashing in her head. If it wasn't Christmas...

But it was Christmas. Gran and Pa were waiting. She had no choice.

But other factors were starting to niggle now. Behind Max, she could see tiny Phoebe lying in her too-big cot. She'd pushed herself out of her swaddle and was waving her tiny hands in desperation. Her face was red with screaming.

She was so tiny. She needed to be hugged, cradled, told all was right with her world. Despite herself, Sunny's heart twisted.

But to forgo Christmas? *No way.*

'I can't,' she told him, still hugging her chocolates. But then she met Max's gaze. This man was in charge of his world but he looked...desperate. The pressure in her head was suddenly overwhelming.

And she made a decision. What she was about to say was ridiculous, crazy, but the sight of those tiny waving arms, that red, desperate face was doing something to her she didn't understand and the words were out practically before she knew she'd utter them.

'Here's my only suggestion,' she told them. 'If you really do want my help... My Gran and Pa live in a big old house in the outer suburbs. It's nothing fancy; in fact it's pretty much falling down. They were caretakers for years and the owner left them lifetime occupancy. It might be dilapidated but it's huge. Daisy and Sam don't live there any more; they live with their partners. Tom and Chloe live in university colleges—blessedly they both have scholarships—so they're home over the summer break, but there's still plenty of room. So no, Mr Grayland, I won't spend Christmas here with you, but if you're desperate, if you truly think you can't manage Phoebe alone, then you're welcome to join us until you can make other arrangements. I'll check with Gran and Pa but I'm sure they'll say yes. They've welcomed waifs and strays before and they've never said no. So, Mr Grayland, that's my only offer. You can stay here and take care of Phoebe yourself, you can make other arrangements or you can come home with me. Take it or leave it.'

Max Grayland was a man accustomed to control. Complete control. He'd been that way almost since birth. Absent parents, a succession of nannies, a succession of strange apartments, homes, hotels and then boarding schools, had seen him develop a shell that was pretty near impermeable. He lived a self-contained, independent life where everything was ordered. He had the means, the staff and the will to ensure all stayed that way.

This woman—this cleaning lady—was asking if he'd step into a world he knew nothing of and wished to know less. A dilapidated house somewhere in the suburbs. Her grandparents and whoever and whatever else might be there.

He was being classified as…a waif or stray?

He was in his pristine hotel penthouse. He had room service at his beck and call. He had his bed, his desk, his work.

But he had a baby who was red in the face from screaming. The childminder had finished her shift at four. She'd fed her, put her into her cot and left her asleep. He'd thought he could cope.

Phoebe had been screaming now for an hour. She wouldn't take another bottle. She'd arched back in his arms, seemingly desperate, and he didn't have one clue what to do about it.

He stood staring at the woman in the doorway, with her bland offer of help. It was ridiculous. There had to be other options.

'Could you take Phoebe home with you?' he asked and her eyes widened in incredulity. And anger.

'Are you kidding? What do you know about me?'

'I assume the hotel will vouch for you.'

'I was hired as a cleaner, not a childcare professional. Would you really do that? Hand your baby over to a stranger?'

'I've watched you care for her. You're good.'

'And how do you know I don't come from a house full of drunken louts and rotting garbage?'

'Miss Raye!' The manager sounded appalled, but Sunny wasn't focused on the manager.

'I don't,' Max said stiffly.

'Is that why you won't come yourself? But you'll send your sister?'

'I…okay. Bad idea,' he managed. 'I hadn't thought it through.'

'Obviously. The offer was both of you or nothing. You seem to be all this little one has, and I'm not interfering in that for the world.'

'What, you're forcing us to bond?'

'I'm not forcing you to do anything. I'm going home.'

And Max Grayland's world suddenly moved to full-blown panic.

She was leaving. The hotel manager would walk out too. He'd be left…not with *this*. With his sister.

You seem to be all this little one has.

Sunny's words resonated in his head. So did the screams behind him. Or were they sobs? Phoebe had been crying for so long she was sounding exhausted. He'd walked the floor with her, tried to feed her again—for heaven's sake, he'd even tried rocking and singing. The next few days stretched ahead, frightening with their lack of help.

What were his options?

Option one: stay here and hope the screams

settled, hope he'd be able to feed her, calm her, keep her alive until Tuesday. The prospect had him terrified.

Option two: take her to the nearest hospital. Say her mother had dumped her and he couldn't cope. The authorities would surely step in, hand her to a professional whose job it was to care for abandoned children.

Abandoned.

Sunny was watching him. He could read the condemnation in her eyes. She knew what he was thinking? *What the...?*

So...option three. Throw himself into the unknown. Go with the hotel cleaner to a Christmas with people he'd never met, to an environment he had no idea of. To lose control.

But he was out of control now, and Sunny was watching.

And he thought suddenly of the slivers he knew of this woman's background. Abandonment had been in this girl's past too, he thought. She knew it and somehow he knew she was expecting the same for Phoebe.

So now, seeing the condemnation on her face—or was it resignation?—he had no choice.

'Can you stop her screaming?' he asked. 'For now? While I think?'

She gave him a hard, assessing look and then she sighed. Laying her precious chocolates on the hall table, she walked to the cot, adjusted the swaddle and lifted Phoebe into her arms. Tucking the baby's head under her chin, she cradled her so she was almost moulded against her. Then she rocked, rubbing her back, crooning a faint tune barely audible to the men watching.

The sobs were still there, but Sunny seemed oblivious. She crooned and rubbed and rocked and crooned and rubbed...

And then Phoebe belched. It was a belch to make a grown man proud. It was a belch that stunned both watching men.

The baby's eyes widened as if she'd shocked herself that she could possibly make such a noise.

And then her eyelids drooped, her tiny head curved into Sunny's soft neck—and she was asleep.

'I'm thinking your childminder was in a hurry when she fed her,' Sunny said as the silence stretched on and the two men watched the magic in amazement. 'A too fast bottle, no burping and the crying will have made things worse. She should be right now.'

'Until when?' Max demanded, incredulous at this small display of magic.

'I have no idea,' Sunny said truthfully. 'Shall I put her back in the cot?'

Max Grayland was known throughout the finance world for his intelligence, his instant assessment of risk, his capacity to make fast decisions that almost always turned out right.

He was so far out of his comfort zone that he felt as if he were drowning, but he was facing three options. The first was to keep this baby and have her wake again the moment Sunny left. The second was to abandon her to social services... Yeah, he could. After all, what did she have to do with him? A token blood relationship?

But Sunny was looking at him, waiting for an answer, and he could read exactly what she thought of him.

So what? She was a hotel cleaner.

She was a hotel cleaner holding a baby who looked exactly like the photographs he'd seen of himself as a newborn.

She was a feisty, warm woman, with skill and humour, and she'd offered him a place at her Christmas table.

So...

So Max Grayland made his decision. He shook his head and moved to stand between Sunny and the cot.

'Let's not put her down,' he told her. 'If I could accept your offer...if it's still on the table...?'

Sunny looked at him, wary now. 'I guess.'

'I'll pay for my accommodation,' he told her. 'Hotel rates.'

'Wait until you see the accommodation before you say that.' And was that laughter behind her eyes?

No matter. Decision made, he was moving on.

He turned back to the hotel manager. 'Could you hold this room for me? I'll return on Tuesday and I'll need professional full-time childcare. I'm not sure how long for—I imagine the legalities will take time to work through. Meanwhile, could you arrange a limousine to take me, Miss Raye and… and Phoebe to wherever Miss Raye directs? With baby supplies?'

'You're really going with her?' the manager demanded, stunned.

'Do I have a choice?' Max said drily. 'I appear to have none, and Miss Raye, believe it or not, I'm grateful.'

CHAPTER FIVE

MAX HAD RESERVATIONS before he arrived at the house. When the hotel limousine pulled into the driveway of Sunny's grandparents' home he very nearly demanded the driver pull out again.

This was like something out of a Gothic novel— in an Australian setting. All it needed was a Halloween moon and a couple of witches hovering overhead on broomsticks to make the picture complete.

It was a ramshackle, tumbledown mansion, or maybe not a mansion, just a house that had been extended upward and outward at random, that had had balconies and turrets added as an afterthought, and had been almost swallowed by the mass of bushland growing right up to the rickety verandas.

It was a wilderness in the middle of suburbia, a house set on a huge block that had been allowed to grow wild.

'Don't tell me,' Sunny said, seeing his look as he unfolded his long frame from the car and looked disbelievingly at what was before him. 'The letter box could do with a splash of paint.'

And he couldn't suppress it. He chuckled and Sunny grinned back at him.

'Yep. Awful. But it's home. Gran and Pa have been caretakers here for fifty years. Miss Murchison passed away almost twenty years ago and left them life tenancy. It's a double-edged sword. It's been fabulous to live in but there's no money to maintain it. I do my best but...'

'You...?'

'Gran and Pa are getting on now and the kids are all busy. So, as I said, the letter box needs painting. Ignore it though and come inside. I texted Gran and she's expecting us.'

And, as if on cue, the front door swung wide. A stout little lady peered out at them and then waved wildly. 'Come on in,' she called, beaming. 'Everyone's here for dinner. Bring the man in, Sunny, and let's meet this baby.'

After that, it turned into a confused mass of faces, noise, laughter. Max struggled to get names. There were Sunny's brothers and sisters, Daisy, Sam, Chloe and a gap-toothed Tom. There were assorted boyfriends and girlfriends and a few general hangers-on. More importantly, there were Ruby and John, Sunny's grandparents. Ruby seemed cheerful, bustling, full of Christmas energy, but it was obvious John wasn't well. Frail and wizened, he sat in state at the head of the dining table. His seat was a wheelchair. He welcomed Max with quiet dignity and apologised for not rising, but he beamed on the noisy proceedings with pride.

And Sunny was everywhere. She showed Max to a room close to the kitchen. 'It's officially the sunroom now, but Daisy used to sleep here and it still has a bed. It's close to the kitchen so we can hear Phoebe.' She sorted the borrowed baby gear and then scooped Phoebe back from Ruby, who'd been cooing over her, and settled her into her new bed. She set up the baby monitor. She then towed the almost speechless Max back to the dining room, demanded the crowd make room, wedged him between Daisy and Tom and then bustled on.

Dinner was a barbecue of sorts. Tom and Sam were officially in charge but were distracted so a stream of blackened sausages were making their unsteady way to the table. No one worried. There were mounds of fresh bread, vast bowls of simple salads, huge bowls of strawberries—'Picked this morning,' Daisy announced proudly—an ocean of cream and a myriad of assorted treats each guest had brought to contribute.

Sunny was busy around the table, making sure plates were filled, reloading empty bowls, refilling glasses, nagging the boys to check the sausages—the standard of cooking did seem to have improved since she'd arrived—and gently chiding her grandfather to eat. All unobtrusively. The family hardly seemed to notice. Ruby seemed to have relaxed the moment Sunny arrived. It was obvious the responsibility for making things work pretty much devolved onto Sunny.

And Max thought of the last thirty-six hours. He thought of Sunny as he'd first seen her, on her knees scrubbing his bathroom floor. A double shift. How many floors had she scrubbed in the last two days? And last night… She'd been up and down to Phoebe. She'd slept on a hard settee with no pillows. She'd woken to another shift of cleaning today.

She was cheerful, happy, laughing and her gaze was everywhere. She was worrying about her Grandpa. She was making sure the myriad guests—including him—felt welcome.

He looked closer and saw shadows under her eyes and wondered if they were always there.

All her siblings seemed much younger than she was. He wondered if they noticed the shadows.

There was little he could do about it. He was wedged between Tom and Daisy. Once they realised he was American they launched into basketball talk. He knew enough to keep his end up, and the rest of the table joined in. As the strawberries were finished he was challenged to throw some hoops, which was the signal for everyone to head outside.

'I'll open Phoebe's window so she can be heard outside but I'll hear her from the kitchen,' Sunny told him.

'She's my responsibility.' He was so at sea here.

'So as soon as she wakes she's over to you, but meanwhile you've been challenged.'

'You're not coming outside yourself?'

'Are you kidding? I have a turkey to stuff, gifts to wrap...'

'I could help.'

'No need. Off you go, kids, and enjoy yourselves.'

So that was how she saw him? One of the kids? One of her responsibilities? But he had little choice but to be ushered outside.

Out the back was the remains of an ancient tennis court. Long ago someone had attached hoops to trees growing at either end. The ground was pitted with tree roots, but that didn't stop a long and very rowdy game being played between makeshift teams.

Max had gym shoes—when did he ever travel without them?—and tossing a basketball was one of his life skills. It was a skill that he'd practised as a teenager with little else to fill his time. He'd never played competitively but the gym had him toned.

'Yay, Max,' was the call as the game was declared over. Thirty-seven to twenty-nine, and twelve of the thirty-seven goals had been his.

And suddenly he was thinking of what he could be doing tonight. Back in New York he'd be well into the company accounts by now. And if he'd been alone at the hotel with Phoebe... *Whoa*, that didn't bear thinking of.

He'd buried his father this morning and the

death was still a heavy weight. It'd probably take years to come to terms with his relationship with the old man. Added to that, he was still shocked to the core by Phoebe's arrival, but tonight had given him time out.

He wondered if Sunny knew it. If she knew she'd given him a gift.

The kids were dispersing. Boyfriends and girlfriends were leaving, Daisy and Sam with them. 'But we'll be back tomorrow,' they called and whooped their way out onto the road to collect their myriad cars and head home. Chloe and Tom headed to their rooms to sleep or do last-minute wrapping. Sunny had appeared momentarily halfway through the game to help Ruby take John to bed, so they were gone too.

Sunny.

He headed to the kitchen and found her sitting by the kitchen range, feeding Phoebe.

The sight of her was almost a physical jolt.

She hadn't had time to change since she'd arrived home. She was still in the jeans and T-shirt she'd put on before she left the hotel.

That she'd been cooking was obvious. A mountainous turkey was under a mesh cover on the bench, stuffed and trussed, ready to go into the oven in the morning. A load of fresh baked mince pies sat on cooling trays and another tray of pastry cases was waiting to be filled.

She had bowls out on the table. A whisk. Eggs. Cream. Brandy.

She'd obviously been interrupted mid-bake by Phoebe's need for a feed. She had smudges of flour on her face. Her curls had flour in as well, and her clothes…

'Yeah, I'm a messy cook,' she said and grinned at him and that jolt turned into something he had no hope of identifying. She looked…

Nope. He had no descriptor. He only knew that the sight of her, flour-coated, no make-up, shadowed, holding his baby sister, smiling up at him— it did something to him that he'd never felt before.

'You won,' she said, still smiling, and he thought yeah, he'd won and he hadn't even heard Phoebe. He'd been out there competing for inconsequential hoops while Sunny had taken over everything else.

He glanced through to the dining room, which two hours ago had been sketchily cleared. It was now transformed, covered with a faded lace tablecloth, glassware, cutlery, bonbons, a tangle of crimson bottle brush acting as a Christmas centrepiece…

She must have done this too.

'It gets a bit busy in the morning,' she told him, following his gaze. 'Gran loves us all to go to church so I like to get ahead. The basketball kept them all outside and gave me space. Thank you.'

She was thanking him?

He was feeling about two inches high. That she'd done all this—and now fed his...fed Phoebe.

'I should have heard her,' he said weakly and there was that smile again. It really was an extraordinary smile. There were dimples right where dimples should be. A smudge of flour lay on the right dimple and he could just...

Or not. Did he want to be tossed out into the snow for Christmas? Or into whatever Australians decreed was their outdoor norm at this time of year?

'It's a lovely warm night so you'd be fine if we threw you out,' she said, still smiling. 'But it's not hot, hooray. I can eat loads more when it's not hot.'

What the...? Had she guessed what he was *thinking?*

Was she fey?

'And you couldn't have heard her because she didn't cry,' she continued, as if she hadn't just poleaxed him. 'I checked and she was snuffling, so I thought I'd get in first. Much better to feed her before she gets distressed, don't you think?'

'I...yes.' He didn't have a clue. 'Could I take her?' he asked weakly. 'I should feed her. You obviously have things to do.'

'Well, I do,' she agreed and that smile appeared again, but it was a weary smile. 'I should say yes. You two need to bond. But you know what? I'm sitting down and I haven't sat down for a while.

How about you make the brandy sauce while I supervise?'

'Me?' he said, stunned. 'Cook…?'

'Under direction,' she said severely. 'You needn't think I'm leaving something so vital to a novice.'

'But…'

'But what?'

He looked at the way her arms cradled the baby. He looked at her stained clothes. He looked at the shadows under her eyes, at the straggles of curls wisping across her forehead and he knew the weariness he'd heard in her voice was bone-deep. How much did this woman have to cope with, and how much more had he added to it by agreeing to come here?

For the first time he thought of this Christmas from her perspective, not his. The young adults around her were in the oblivious land of adolescence. Her Gran, cheerful but frail herself, seemed fully occupied in caring for her John. He'd seen Sunny helping there too, her assistance almost inconspicuous, but obviously needed.

This ancient tumbledown house…this tangled garden… It felt good, it felt a home, but how much of that was due to one slip of a girl? A woman, he reminded himself, because Sunny was every inch a woman. A woman who was asking him to make brandy sauce, under her direction, while she cared for his child.

His child.

It…*she*…wasn't his, he told himself but the thought slammed back in response. If she wasn't his then whose was she? Would she be put up for adoption? For some reason every instinct rebelled.

His father's estate would surely provide for her—legally, it must. As his father's executor he'd need to set up a base, employ a nanny, make sure she was provided with all material necessities until she came of age.

He looked again at Sunny. She was smiling down into Phoebe's little face, tender, caring.

Where would he find a nanny like this? His experience with nannies had been bleak, moved from parent to parent, from place to place. Time after time he remembered… 'Get over it, Max, she's only a nanny. We'll find someone else at the next place. Oh, for heaven's sake, boy, stop snivelling. You don't cry over a hired hand.'

To be raised by…hired hands?

Phoebe was facing the same path.

'So will you be making the brandy sauce or not?' Sunny asked mildly and he forced his mind away from a future that suddenly seemed inordinately bleak and focused on the here and now. He needed to help this woman who'd pulled him out of short-term trouble, at some cost to herself.

'I can try,' he said bravely and she grinned.

'What a hero. You know how to separate eggs?'

'I…no.'

'Then you're about to learn. We keep chooks so we have plenty. What a good thing! Okay, Mr Grayland, pinny on.'

'Pinny?'

'That's a very nice shirt,' she told him. 'To say nothing of the fact that you're still wearing your suit pants. They wouldn't go well with brandy sauce. Pinnies are behind the pantry door. The pink one's mine but there's one behind it the boys use for barbecuing. It says "The Man, The Myth, The Legend". See if you can prove it right.'

It took him five shots before he got an egg separated without contaminating the white with broken yolk.

'That's okay. I'll sieve the shell out and use them to make quiche on Boxing Day,' Sunny said serenely.

'So what happens if yolk gets into the white?'

'The white doesn't fluff. How can you make brandy sauce without fluff?'

For heaven's sake... He thought briefly of the massive financial decisions waiting for him in his briefcase, and here he was, worrying about fluff.

But it seemed important, mostly because Sunny was waiting for him to succeed. He was being measured by fluff.

He cracked the next egg and managed to get the yolk in one container and the white in the bowl.

Yay for him.

'Don't crack the next egg over the same bowl,' Sunny told him. 'Use a mug and tip the white in the bowl when you succeed. You don't want to contaminate what you've done.'

There was a comparison he could make—isolating financial deals so success or failure didn't drag others down.

Not so different really. Their worlds.

He glanced at the flour-smudged Sunny, holding the now sleeping baby, and he thought, *Who am I kidding?*

He messed another egg. Badly.

'Concentrate,' Sunny said severely. 'Brandy sauce is important.'

It was. Mostly because he could block out tomorrow and the day after that and all the days following while he focused on whipping egg white and creaming yolks and sugar and whipping cream and then adding brandy bit by bit. *'We wouldn't want to overdo it and make it curdle, but there's nothing worse than a not-very-brandyish brandy sauce.'*

He finished. Sunny ordered that he pour two small glasses—just to test. He tested and it was magnificent.

Phoebe slept. Outside the wind was stirring the massive eucalypts around the house, and a kookaburra was making a late-night complaint.

How far was he from New York? This was another universe.

Sunny was smiling into the sleeping face of baby Phoebe, her face gentler, younger, almost free.

Two different universes… They'd collided and what on earth was he going to do about it?

Sunny's room was just down the hall from the room Max and Phoebe were sharing. She heard Phoebe wake at two and was out in the kitchen preparing the bottle before Max emerged.

He had no hotel dressing gown here. He was wearing boxers and nothing else. The sight took her aback. He stood, looking half asleep, in the doorway, blinking in the harsh kitchen light.

He was carrying Phoebe.

Almost naked man, holding baby. *It's a cliché,* Sunny told herself. *It's a set-up designed to slam under every female's defences and I'm no exception.*

'Take her back to the bedroom,' she managed. 'I'll bring the bottle.'

'I'll feed her here…'

'Feed her in the half dark. She needs to start delineating night and day as soon as possible. Go on, get her out of the light.'

'Yes, ma'am,' he said in a strange voice but he left. Two minutes later she knocked and entered his bedroom. He was perched on the windowsill. The window was open and the room was moonlit. The silhouette of man and baby framed by the window took her breath away all over again.

'I could have made it myself,' Max told her as she struggled with composure and managed to hand over the bottle.

'You'd have coped in the hotel.'

'I'd have been terrified. Thank you, Sunny. I will make this up to you.'

'It's okay,' she told him in a voice that was none too steady. She needed to back out fast. What was it with this guy? He was so far out of her league he might as well exist on another planet. What was it about the gentleness in his voice that made something inside her twist? Something that had never twisted before…

It's because it's never had time to twist, she told herself, struggling to think practically. Here she was, almost thirty, and she'd never had a proper boyfriend. She'd never had time. Shift work, massive pressures at home, the fact that she'd had practically no schooling and what man would be interested in a woman who hadn't even passed Year Eight…?

'Are you okay?' Max asked, still gentle, and she backed off with a start.

'I…yes. Thank you.'

'It's I who need to thank you.'

'Then you're welcome. Don't forget to burp her. And if she doesn't finish the bottle don't reheat it next time she's hungry. She needs sterilised bottles and newly made formula.'

'Yes, ma'am.'

'And you're right with the nappy?'

'Nappy?'

'Diaper.'

'I am.' He sounded smug. 'I changed her before I came out to the kitchen. Nothing to it.'

'By which you mean it was only wet.'

And he chuckled. He'd popped the teat into his little sister's mouth. Phoebe accepted the teat with eagerness, and started suckling.

This man…this baby…this chuckle…

'I guess I did mean that,' he told her. 'But I'm sure I'll cope when the time comes.' And then he gazed down at the baby in his arms and seemed to change his mind. 'No,' he said. 'I'm not sure I'll cope. I hope I don't need to.'

'You mean you don't want her?' It was none of her business. She should retreat but there was something about this man… Something about this night that made her probe.

'I hope Isabelle will change her mind.'

'I do too,' Sunny admitted. 'But I doubt she will.'

'Why?'

'Because she insisted a porter push the pram. Because she didn't once falter. Because she didn't even look into the pram as she left.'

And Max looked at her for a long, long moment.

She should have dressed, she decided, feeling totally discomfited. She was wearing a shabby nightgown and an even shabbier cardigan. She felt like someone's poor relation.

She needed to back away, but...

'Is that how your mother treated you?' he asked gently. 'Did your mother not look at you, or at your brothers and sisters? Was it you who did all the looking, Sunny Raye?'

She couldn't answer. What sort of question was that, to be asked by a stranger?

'I don't... I have to go now,' she managed at last, suddenly feeling close to tears. Why? What earthly reason did she have to cry? It was just... this man got to her.

No. It was the situation. One more baby left to fend for herself.

'Don't get up the next time she wakes,' Max told her, even more gently, obviously deciding she wouldn't or couldn't answer. 'I'll call you if I need you but I'm sure I can manage. You need sleep.'

'I...yes.' There seemed nothing else to say. 'You could have managed at the hotel.'

'But I didn't have to and I'll be grateful for ever. And Sunny... I pay my debts.'

'There's no debt to pay,' she whispered and her emotions were suddenly too much.

She wasn't emotional—she wasn't. She was pragmatic. Dependable. Unflappable. That was how she'd survived this long and that was how she needed to survive now.

'Indeed there is.' And Max was smiling at her in

such a way she didn't feel the least bit pragmatic, dependable or unflappable. 'Oh, and Sunny...'

'Yes?' She was almost out of the door.

'Merry Christmas,' he told her softly and she stood for a long moment and looked back at him.

'I... Merry Christmas,' she said at last, and bolted.

Phoebe was fast asleep before her bottle was finished but Max had learned his lesson. He set her on his shoulder as he'd seen Sunny do. He walked her back and forth across the room, rubbing her little back with care, and was rewarded by a satisfactory belch. It wasn't nearly as impressive as the one he'd heard back at the hotel but then, Phoebe hadn't begun to be upset yet.

He set her back into her borrowed cot and stood watching her sleep.

He knew nothing about babies. He'd never thought of having a child of his own.

Or maybe he had, but the idea was vague. Some time in the future he might be a parent but the concept was nebulous because the practicalities seemed overwhelming.

He'd need to find a woman he wanted to spend the rest of his life with, which seemed pretty much impossible. He liked his life as a loner. He could do as he pleased, answer to no one, care for no one. And no one would care for him. The thought of someone caring was a bridge too far. He'd let her down or she'd let him down.

He remembered time after time with the nannies. Always leaving.

And then there was the pup given to him when he was eight years old, the dog which for some reason even now seemed the biggest grief of all. But he wasn't going there. All he knew was that attachment hurt. He didn't need it and he didn't want it.

So...marriage without attachment? As if that would happen.

This nebulous partner would no doubt want to share his bed and he'd had enough affairs to realise women didn't like men who worked late, slept briefly and then listened to the world's financial affairs instead of sleeping. He'd head to his desk to check something and they'd wake and want bed talk. But his head would be doing business deals in Switzerland and something would go wrong and he'd need to be on the next plane. He'd leave with apologies but usually all he'd feel was relief.

Which brought him back to one sleeping baby.

If Sunny was right and Isabelle really didn't care, then he was her only family.

The thought was terrifying.

Could he turn his back?

Adoption? There were surely plenty of good,

kind people who were desperate to give a baby a home.

But how could he know who to choose? How could he be sure he was doing the right thing?

And…she was his sister.

Half-sister, he told himself fiercely. He *could* walk away.

As someone had walked away from Sunny Raye.

Why could he not stop thinking of her? She was a hotel cleaner who'd helped him out. Nothing more.

She was a woman who took on the world. He didn't need to be told how much caring for this extended family cost her. He'd watched as her grandparents and her siblings deferred to her, depended on her, loved her.

Where was the room for Sunny Raye in all this? He'd heard the family chatter over the dinner table, of outside lives, of jobs, of studies, of interests. Even John and Ruby had been talking of the cricket, looking forward to the Boxing Day test, remembering past matches and knowing they could settle in front of the telly while Sunny… Sunny went back to scrubbing floors at the hotel.

It wasn't any of his business, he told himself. He'd pay her well for helping out this Christmas and that would help her financial situation. He needed to focus on Phoebe.

Phoebe.

It might be ridiculous to care about such a scrap of a thing after one day but he did and he wasn't about to let her go for adoption. Which meant he had to get the paperwork in order. He needed to find Isabelle and get her permission to take Phoebe from the country. He needed to…adopt her himself?

There was a bag of worms. What would he do with her?

He'd do what his parents had done. He'd find a nanny. He wouldn't move as his parents had moved. He could find a nanny who was likely to stay.

But that'd take time. Even finding Isabelle would take time. The hotel childminder came to mind. He hadn't warmed to the woman. She'd done her job punctiliously but she hadn't cared.

Not like Sunny cared.

And then his mind stopped.

Sunny.

He was seeing her now as he'd first seen her, a cleaning woman on her knees, her uniform stained, her hands worn by years of hard work, scrubbing a stain from the bathroom floor. How many bathroom floors had she scrubbed? And was she due to return to her scrubbing the day after Christmas? He'd seen how she'd responded to the offer of double pay and now he'd seen her home he knew why. Of course she'd be back at work.

But she was good with Phoebe. Awesome.

Did she have a passport?

No matter. Technicalities were what he was good at.

But he'd seen how much the old couple depended on her. Her whole family...

So put your ducks in a row first, he told himself and then he decided he'd tell Phoebe his idea.

'I'll try,' he told his little sister. 'I suspect it can't be permanent but if Sunny will help... Do you agree? Yes? Then let's go for it.'

CHAPTER SIX

CHRISTMAS MORNING. Sunny woke at six and allowed herself a couple of moments of doing nothing at all.

She couldn't hear Phoebe. Max had coped by himself, then. Good.

Except she wouldn't think of him. She had these few precious minutes before the demands of Christmas took over. Tomorrow she'd be heading back to work. Life would start again.

Life. She put her hands behind her head and let herself drift to where she went so often. She tried not to, but as she saw each of her siblings follow their dreams it was hard to avoid.

What if...?

What if she'd had a decent education? What if she didn't have family obligations that took every cent and every moment? What if she wasn't almost thirty and her hands looked like she was seventy and her hair didn't need a cut and she could afford...?

A spa. There was a spectacular spa in the hotel. She saw patrons coming and going, pink and scrubbed, eyes glazed from pampering, from soothing music, from gentle hands...

She knew some of the masseurs. They looked

a little like she did. They were the pamperers, not the pamperees. Just like she was.

But, just for this moment, she let herself lie under the covers and dream that her life could include a spa or two. Or that she could have the life she'd managed to give her siblings. Education. Boyfriends and girlfriends. Fun.

Um, not. Get over it, Sunny, she told herself. *You've done great. You never thought you'd get this far and it's Christmas morning, so get out of bed and do the vegetables before you need to help shower Pa. Before Max needs you to help with Phoebe.*

Max… Phoebe… Okay, she had to think of him a little and why did that worry her? What was it about the man and his baby that had her so unsettled? He was simply a hotel guest she was being kind to.

Except he was gorgeous.

He represented everything she didn't have, she thought, but then she thought it was more than that. His smile… His chuckle… The way he looked at Phoebe.

He could have taken the baby straight to the nearest welfare service, or he could have let the media know and the ensuing storm might have ensured Isabelle would take the baby back. Publicity was Isabelle's reason for existing. She could see Isabelle facing the press, woebegone, all innocence.

I just needed my beautiful daughter's family to acknowledge her existence. She's part of the Grayland dynasty and she's been ignored...

Okay, she didn't know if that was how it would have played out but Max hadn't risked it. He'd accepted responsibility, even though it meant... Christmas with her?

What a sacrifice. Christmas with the cleaning lady.

She found herself smiling. This was fantasy, being landed with a billionaire. For two days.

Okay, one day because she'd be back at work tomorrow. Max would stay on for the extra day, she guessed, because there was no babysitting service at the hotel until after Boxing Day. But Gran could give advice while she was at work and Chloe and Tom didn't start back at their holiday jobs until the day after Boxing Day either. They could look after one little baby. They could even have fun.

And there was that worm again, that niggle of jealousy she spent her life suppressing. Whenever something nice happened she had to work. Or do something else. Nice things happened to other people.

Like Max staying an extra day? Was that nice?

There was a thought that wasn't worth exploring. He was a guy she was being kind to. He was part of her working life.

Speaking of which, she had to get those veggies done. She had a decent veggie garden out the back and she'd been threatening death to anyone who touched a pea for the last week. Therefore they were ripe for picking. She'd left it until this morning so they'd be at their peak.

So get up and pick peas and stop thinking about Max, she told herself fiercely, and threw back the covers and headed for the shower.

Merry Christmas.

Phoebe woke early but Max was already awake. As she started to stir he dressed fast, then headed for the kitchen. He made her bottle quietly so as not to disturb the sleeping house and by the time she opened her mouth to wail he was ready to scoop her up and give her what she needed.

Success!

He sat on the windowsill while he fed her, so he saw Chloe heading off for a run. He had them sorted by now. Chloe was the fourth of the siblings, studying fashion design. She'd been on the opposing basketball team last night, a ball of vibrant energy, and it didn't surprise him to see her running into the dawn. Half an hour later he watched her return, check her time then start to do a wind-down on the back lawn.

Phoebe was still awake, lying sleepily in his arms. He carried his bundle out to meet her.

'Hey, Chloe!'

'Hey,' she said cheerily. 'How's the rug rat?'

'Fed and sleepy. Can I talk to you?'

'Sure.'

Fifteen minutes later they were still sitting on the back step when Sunny emerged. She was wearing old jeans and a stained T-shirt, carrying a colander. She looked like she meant business.

She stopped dead when she saw them.

'Hey.' Chloe jumped up and greeted her big sister with a hug. 'Happy Christmas. It's going to be a gorgeous day. Max and I have been busy making plans.'

'What plans?'

'That'd be telling. Christmas is all about surprises and I'm loving this one. Meanwhile, I promised Kim and Sarah I'd Skype them. They're in London—it's still Christmas Eve over there and I need to catch them before they go clubbing. See you soon.'

She disappeared and Max watched Sunny's face as she watched her go. It was a mixture of pride and resignation—mostly pride, though. He looked again at the colander, at Sunny's working clothes, and he thought, *Does anyone in this family notice?* Last night they'd all played basketball and Sunny had cooked. Now Chloe was Skyping her clubbing friends while Sunny worked again.

'Colander?' he queried but Sunny was stooping to check Phoebe. Making sure he'd kept her alive during the night?

'Great,' she said softly, touching a tiny, sleepy cheek. 'Well done, you.'

And what was in those few words to make his chest swell? He'd kept Phoebe alive overnight without waking Sunny. What a hero!

'I'm glad we didn't need to wake you,' he managed.

'Me too. I was tired.'

You're still tired, he thought, looking at the shadows under her eyes, but somehow he knew those shadows were permanent.

'Colander?' he said again.

'Peas.'

'Peas. Right.'

'In the veggie garden. You want to see?'

'Okay.' He rose and carried the sleepy baby in his arms, following her around to the back of the house.

He hadn't seen this last night. It was a vegetable garden of magnificent proportions. Tomatoes, beans, peas, corn, lettuces, berries—rows of carefully tended crops in all different stages of growth.

Sunny headed for the peas and started picking. With Phoebe in his arms he couldn't help. He watched for a while, stunned at the scale of the garden. 'Who cares for all this?'

'Pa started it decades back,' she told him, picking with the speed of long practice. 'He set it up and loved it. He can't do so much now, though.'

'So it's down to you.'

'The kids don't have time. Every now and then

I bully them to do some weeding or digging, but they have their own lives. You have no idea how much money it saves us, though. Daisy and Sam raid it every time they come home too, so it helps them.'

'They're not self-sufficient?'

'Almost.' He could hear the pride of a parent in her voice. 'Daisy finished physiotherapy last November. She starts her first job this week. She and her boyfriend have just set up a flat together. He's as broke as she is, though, so it's been a struggle. Sam's just finished an IT degree and he's been offered a post-grad scholarship. He's living in at the uni, tutoring to pay expenses. He works in a call centre a couple of nights a week too, so he's almost off my hands. Chloe and Tom…they have a way to go but the end's in sight.'

'And you?'

'Me?'

'What's the end in sight for you?'

'To see them all safe.' She said it solidly, definitely. 'When Mum died and they were all sent to foster homes…you have no idea how terrified I was. I made a vow then and I've kept it.' She caught herself, no doubt hearing the grim determination behind her words, and looked up and gave him a shamefaced grin. 'That sounds like it's been all me and it hasn't. Gran and Pa have been awesome.'

'But what happens after they're safe?' Max asked. 'What happens to Sunny?'

She shook her head. 'Who knows? I haven't been brave enough to look that far ahead.'

'I think you're brave enough to do anything.'

Her colander was full. How fast was she? She took a moment out, split a pod open and ate some peas, then split another and offered it to him. 'Sometimes I am,' she agreed. 'I applied to the best hotel in Sydney for a cleaning job and I can't tell you how much courage that took. The interview made me quake in my boots but I got it. Regular hours. Union negotiated wages. Meal breaks. I'd been doing casual house cleaning until then and the change was heaven. Taste?'

He tasted a freshly opened pea, standing in the garden in the small hours of Christmas morning. There were birds everywhere, raucous in the trees above their heads. Sunny had netted the most vulnerable of the crops but he had a feeling they were being watched, in the hope the netting could be breached.

He didn't blame the birds. This pea was worth fighting for. He glanced across at the splashes of crimson under the netting and Sunny saw where he was looking and grinned.

'The strawberries have had a week's embargo until yesterday too,' she told him. 'These are for tonight's pavlovas, which reminds me, I need to get the pavs into the oven before I need it for the turkey. Can you manage to take the peas inside while I do the watering and let the chooks out? I need to get on.'

Of course she did. He carried Phoebe and the peas back up to the veranda and then stood and watched as Sunny headed down the path towards the hen house.

It'd take more than Chloe, he thought. Tom too? And support from Daisy and Sam.

He needed to knock on a few bedroom doors, he decided, and he needed to do it fast.

Church. Sunny still had nightmares of the year her mother had died, the year the world had seemed irredeemably shattered and her siblings had been cast into the separate paths of foster care. But then the social workers had found Gran and Pa, and miraculously they'd been enfolded with love. That Christmas, for the first time, Gran and Pa had played Santa Claus and there'd been a gift for Sunny.

She'd stood in church that first Christmas morning and she'd held Gran's hand and she'd wept. For some reason, every Christmas since then she'd felt the same way.

Everyone she cared about was with her now. The kids knew how important this was, to her and to Gran and Pa. Pa sat at the end of the pew in his wheelchair. Would he be here next Christmas? The thought made her cringe but she put it away.

She was here to count her blessings, as she did every Christmas.

The only problem was, this Christmas she had a distraction—a large one—sitting beside her.

For, as the family had readied for church, Gran had rounded on Max. 'We've ordered the maxi-taxi to take us. That gives us room for John's wheelchair so there's room for you and for Phoebe.'

'Phoebe might cry,' Max had protested and it was true. She'd been fed again but she was restless.

'And if the lot of us can't dandle one baby between us there's something wrong,' Pa had declared, so now Phoebe was still awake, nestled in his arms but seemingly content, gazing upward as if trying to make sense of this man who was holding her.

This man sitting beside Sunny.

They were sitting at the end of the pew, in case Phoebe decided to roar and they had to take her out. The kids were on the far side of Sunny. Gran and Pa were in the pew in front so his wheelchair could sit in the aisle.

Gran and Pa, holding hands.

Sunny and Max and baby Phoebe.

Family.

Anyone looking at her and Max might think… might think…

Don't go there, Sunny thought, as the Christmas sermon stretched on, but how could she not? Fantasy?

But this was a fantasy. There'd never been time or space for her to think of a love life and, besides, who'd want her?

She gazed down at her hands, at the lines and calluses formed by years of hard manual work, at the cracked, blunt nails, at the absence of rings. She stretched them out for just a moment and suddenly, astonishingly, Max's fingers were closing over hers.

'Good hands,' he said in a low voice. 'Honourable hands.'

She should pull away. She should...

Okay, she didn't know what she should do. Had he known what she was thinking? How many hands had this man seen that looked like hers? None. She knew it.

She should tug her hand back from his and the contact would be over. That would be the sensible course, the only course, but she couldn't quite manage it. His clasp was warm and strong. Good.

Fantasy enveloped her again for a moment, insidious in its sweetness. To keep sitting here, to feel the peace of this moment, this place, this man...

The organ murmured and then soared into the introduction of *Silent Night*.

It needed only this, she thought wildly. Her favourite carol. Her entire family safe and happy. A billionaire to-die-for. A perfect baby...

And then the perfect baby opened her mouth and squawked, and Tom on the other side of her noticed where her hand was and dug her hard in the ribs. He grinned and waggled his eyebrows. The congregation was rising to its feet and starting to sing.

And Sunny tugged her hand from Max. She took the wailing Phoebe from him and propped her on her shoulder and rubbed her back. Phoebe subsided. Sunny looked firmly down at the printed words Tom was holding for her—she needed something to look at rather than Max—and she started to sing too.

She'd had moments like this before, she told herself. Moments of fantasy. But they were just that—fantasy. She was indeed blessed with her family, so what was she doing dreaming of more?

And then she realised why Phoebe hadn't been sleeping and what was behind the wail.

'Phew...' Tom gasped and Sunny winced.

'I'll take her,' Max said and for a moment she almost let him. But the fantasy had her unsettled. She needed to ground herself fast and what better way than a nappy change?

'I've agreed to take on responsibilities today,' she whispered. 'If I were you I'd soak it up because after Christmas she's all yours.'

Max didn't sing. Instead he stood and listened as the music swelled around him. He watched

Sunny's family; they hadn't realised Sunny had slipped out. Like last night playing basketball… Sunny was out of sight, in the background, working to make them happy.

She deserved his Christmas gift.

Would she accept?

He could only hope.

Max might be pretty much a hermit where Christmas was concerned but he wasn't completely isolated. He usually emerged from his self-inflicted solitude for Christmas dinner, sharing it with like-minded souls in the restaurant near his apartment. The menu was always stunning, oysters maybe, caviar, turkey with truffle stuffing, an elegant modern take on plum pudding… The wines would be breathtakingly excellent. There'd be exquisite Swiss truffles with coffee, with cognac and the finest of Cuban cigars for those inclined.

This Christmas dinner was about as far from that as it was possible to be. There was no entrée—just a turkey so big it took two of the boys to carry it to the table. Sausage and herb stuffing, mounds of potato mash, a vast jug of gravy, and bowls of vegetables and salads. There was no elegance—it was a cheerful free-for-all.

Max found he wasn't missing his oysters and truffle-stuffing one bit.

Then there was the pudding and there was no modern take here. 'I've handed the recipe to Sunny now and she's done us proud,' Ruby told him, beaming. 'You're the guest; you light it.' So with the family watching—with a certain amount of anxiety—he followed Ruby's instructions, heating the brandy and then flaming the pudding. They'd pulled the blinds closed and the flames lit the room.

Then the pudding was taken firmly from him—apparently he might be trusted to light it but only Ruby was going to serve. 'Cream, ice cream or brandy sauce?' Ruby asked but the question was met with howls of derision.

'He may live half a world away but the man's not stupid,' Sunny declared. 'Give him all three.'

So he had all three and came back for more. And Sunny grinned at him as she watched him pour more of the truly wonderful brandy sauce and he thought...

Um...not. Was the brandy sauce going to his head? There was no reason his thoughts were suddenly wandering in impossible directions.

'And now's the best part.' It was Tom, the youngest. 'Presents! Where's Phoebe? She has to be included.'

Phoebe was in the next room, sleeping soundly, but her presence was deemed essential. Sunny brought her in as they headed to the living room—and the Christmas tree. She handed the baby over to Max and he sat and held her as the family swapped gifts.

These weren't big gifts. His cherry liqueur chocolates were the largest offering of all, greeted with stunned delight from Ruby and hoots of laughter from everyone else.

'She always hides them in her knicker drawer,' Sunny told him. 'We've given her a conundrum. The box is too big.'

'The knickers will have to go,' Ruby declared, clutching her precious box. 'And now here's something for you and Phoebe.'

For him... He accepted a parcel wrapped in brown paper and tied with an obviously recycled crimson ribbon.

Things were getting a bit much. He wasn't used to this kind of personal. To say he was out of his comfort zone would be putting it mildly.

'Open it,' Sunny told him and somehow he balanced a sleeping Phoebe while he unfastened the wrapping.

It was a sock. An old sock, by the look of things, black, with a toe that was almost worn through, but it had been transformed.

It had embroidered eyes, nose and a wide crimson smile. Great bushy eyebrows were made with brown wool, as was its hair. The two toe ends had been tied to make waggly ears.

'Sunny made all the kids a Mr Sock when they were little and we decided Phoebe needed one too,' Ruby told him. 'You can use him to tell her stories. Starting now. Kids are never too young to hear stories.'

And he glanced at Sunny and caught such an expression…

A glimmer of tears?

But the room was suddenly full of laughing conflict.

'My Mr Sock is bigger,' Tom said proudly.

'Yeah, but my Mr Sock's pink.' Daisy gave him a shove. 'Much better.'

'You've all kept your Mr Socks?'

'Why wouldn't we?' Sam demanded. 'Is that the end of the gifts? I hear shortbread calling.'

'There's something more,' Max said. He was still watching Sunny. She was on the floor, surrounded by a sea of wrapping paper, misty-eyed, and he thought she looked…

Yeah, he didn't understand that either. Why the sight of her should do that twisting thing…

'I have a gift for Sunny,' he said and got nods of conspiratorial pleasure from everyone except Sunny, who looked confused.

'I don't need…'

'No,' he said softly. 'But you deserve. You might not wish to accept it, though. Try it and see.' And he took a folded slip of paper from his back pocket and handed it over.

She flicked it open and read it—and looked even more confused.

'It's…an airline ticket. Sydney to New York.'

She read the detail, looking increasingly bewildered. 'First class. And there's no date.' She stared up at him. 'Max, I can't take this. I can't...'

'You can,' he said gently. 'But, before you accept or decline, you need to know there's a catch. It's not a freebie.'

'I don't understand.'

'I need a childminder.' And then, as she opened her mouth to tell him all the reasons that was a crazy idea, he held up his hand. 'Give me a moment. Let me explain.'

What he really wanted was space, privacy to explain his carefully thought-out plan, but in this weird old house, surrounded by family and all the trappings of Christmas—and knowing his idea would never get off the ground without the enthusiasm of everyone—he needed to say it now.

'You're not a childminder.' In truth, he wasn't sure what she was—she'd stopped seeming like a cleaner and he didn't have a job description to replace it with. 'But you work for the most prestigious hotel in Sydney. Ruby says you value your job and wouldn't want to lose it. So this morning I rang the manager. He was able to make an executive decision—and that decision is to grant you leave without pay for the next few weeks. I'll make a donation to compensate them for the loss of someone who must surely rate as one of their best employees.'

She was staring at him as if he'd grown two heads. 'You rang the manager? About me?'

'I told him he has gold. I told him you're astoundingly undervalued.'

'No!' She sounded panicked. 'That's my job. You can't…'

'Sunny, hear me out.' His gaze met hers and held. He was willing reassurance into his gaze, confidence, trustworthiness—everything he most needed her to see. 'Sunny, firstly I have not jeopardised your job in any way. That's a promise. However, I have a proposition, and all I've done is make it possible for you to accept if you wish. Sunny, I'm intending to take Phoebe back to the States as soon as possible. There are bureaucratic issues but if Isabelle's still insistent that she doesn't want her then I can pull a legal team together and make things happen fast. So, for the next week or so, I'd ask that I base myself here. Ruby and John have already said we're welcome. Then…' he hesitated, because this was the biggie '…then I'd ask that you travel back to New York with me. I'd ask that you stay for a month. Help me settle her into a routine. And help me employ a nanny.'

'Hey, that's all work,' Tom said, as Sunny stared at him as if he'd lost his mind. 'Full-time childcare doesn't sound like fun. We thought…'

'That the deal was better than that?' Max nodded. 'I hope it is.' Still Max was watching Sunny.

'I have a large apartment overlooking Central Park. I also have a housekeeper. Eliza will cook and clean and I'm sure she'll also take care of Phoebe for a few hours each day. Sunny, you'll have time off to explore New York. You'll also have an open-ended credit card, to see shows, museums, to shop…'

'You're giving her an open-ended credit card to shop?' Chloe squeaked, full of little-sister glee. 'Sunny, you could…'

'Shop for Sunny,' Max said firmly, grinning as he saw where Chloe's mind was headed. 'Any size fifteen basketball boots or clubbing heels meant for…oh, maybe a fashion student won't get past my eagle-eyed inspection.' And then he looked at Sunny and he glanced again at Phoebe's Mr Sock. 'But it won't be very eagle-eyed. Sunny, I want you to have fun and I know gifts would give you pleasure.'

But Sunny was still looking thunderstruck. 'Max, I can't. You know I can't. This is…'

'A cruel offer if I didn't mean it,' he agreed. 'But I do mean it. My housekeeper's part-time. She can take care of Phoebe a little but not for full days. I need to get back to work and Phoebe needs a constant until I can find her a nanny. I have no idea what to look for in a good nanny but I suspect you do. And, before you hit me with all the other reasons you can't come, your grandparents and brothers and sisters and I have been talking.'

'What, all of you?'

'Serially, not in a bunch,' Tom said gleefully. 'Wait till you hear, Sun.'

'It's awesome,' Chloe added but he shook his head to silence both of them. Once again he wished he could take her somewhere private. The look on her face was worrying him. She looked… terrified.

'It's okay,' he said gently. 'No one's bullying you. But your grandparents tell me January is holiday month in Australia. The universities are closed, which means Chloe and Tom are staying here. That means they can help your grandparents at night. But they also have holiday jobs. Tom's pulling beer at the local pub and Chloe's working retail at the Christmas sales. They tell me they need the jobs for the family to survive, but I've offered them alternatives. The plan is for them to quit and stay here.'

'And help Gran take care of Pa, and work in the garden and even paint the letter box,' Chloe announced. 'Though why the letter box seems important…' She grinned, shrugged and continued. 'No matter. We'll be doing everything you usually do, Sunny, only more because it'll be our full-time job, and the truly amazing thing is that Max will pay. He's offered what we were getting as a holiday job plus fifty per cent. Fifty per cent! Oh, plus the work on Tom's teeth. He must really

want you, Sunny. He must think you're as awesome as we do.'

'But I'm not awesome,' Sunny said in a small
voice. 'I'm…' She faltered and shook her head.
'New York…' She said it as if it was outer space.

'Will you come?'

'You'd spend all that money on me?' She
glanced at Tom then, at the gap where he'd fallen
skateboarding and broken a tooth. 'On us?'

'I'm rich in my own right,' he said gently.
'But my father was obscenely rich and I'll use
his money if it'll make you feel better. This is
about Phoebe. His daughter deserves the best care
money can buy.'

'I'm not even trained.'

'I can't believe you can say that. Your family
seems to think you almost single-handedly raised
them. You coped on your own for years, and if
that's not training in childcare I don't know what
is.'

'You can get the best…'

'I know the best when I see it. You're the best.'

She stared at him and then stared wildly at
Ruby. 'Gran…'

And Gran grinned. 'My mother used to tell me
never to look a gift horse in the mouth and if
Max isn't a gift horse I don't know what is. Just
say yes.'

'A gift horse…' She practically choked.

'Exactly.' Ruby beamed. 'And Max promised

that your ticket's open-ended so you can come home any time you need.' She was suddenly stern. 'So if this apartment isn't big enough to be separate and if you feel you're being pushed...to do anything you're not happy with...'

'She means if he pushes you to be his mistress,' Tom said, leering evilly, and Daisy kicked him.

'She mightn't mind being his mistress,' Chloe added and moved out of the range of Daisy's feet fast.

But Sunny wasn't noticing. To say she looked stunned would be an understatement.

'So agree,' Ruby said, beaming. 'And then we can all take a nice nap and then get on with filling the pavlovas for tea.'

'I can't...'

'You can't take it all in,' Max said swiftly. The last thing he wanted was a panicked no. 'Think about it and we'll talk later. Then you can tell me your qualms and I can tell you the ways I've solved them.'

'What a hero,' Daisy said and grinned and the whole family was grinning—apart from Sunny.

'I'm not a hero,' Max said. 'I'm an ordinary guy who needs help.'

'An ordinary billionaire with a baby,' Chloe added. 'Go for it, our Sunny. You might just have a ball.'

CHAPTER SEVEN

CHRISTMAS TEA. Leftovers and pavlova. It was her favourite meal of the year, Sunny thought, but this year she hardly tasted it.

As the tea things were cleared, yet another basketball session was mooted. Once again Sunny stayed on the sidelines. In truth she'd never learned to toss a hoop—she'd never seemed to have time—but she loved watching them.

But now she was watching Max have fun with her family. She was watching the kids fall under his spell and she thought, *That's what it is. A spell.*

He had her mesmerised and it scared her. His proposition scared her.

When she heard Phoebe fussing again it was almost a relief. She slipped away from the game, gathered the baby in her arms and carried her out onto the path leading up to the hills beyond.

This was a suburban setting but bushland had been preserved. There were parrots in the flowering gums that lined the streets, squawking a cacophony that was almost a part of her. The houses were all set well back, with trees between street and house. Discreet Christmas tableaux decorated the yards but the streets were deserted. The tableaux seemed almost out of place now that Christmas was done.

But was Christmas done? She walked and crooned as Phoebe fussed and she thought about Max's extraordinary gift. She really thought about it.

What she needed to do, she decided, was to take Max out of the equation. Because her first thought as she'd opened the envelope and seen the tickets was... *He wants to take me to New York.*

Which was a dumb thing to think. He wanted to hand Phoebe over and for some reason he'd decided he could trust her.

He had the money to pay whatever it took. So why not go?

New York...

She'd never been on an aeroplane. She'd never even managed to get interstate.

This was a once-in-a-lifetime chance.

So take it.

It scared her.

Why? She'd faced down many things in her life—her mother's drunken rages, desertion, loss, far too much responsibility. She'd coped with everything and she hadn't flinched. She prided herself on her strength. Indeed, sometimes it was the only thing she had to cling to.

So why was she scared?

She knew why. It was because of her initial reaction to those tickets. Because she'd suddenly thought, *He wants me*. The thought had been fleeting, short-lived, ridiculous, but it had her deeply unsettled.

She thought of Tom's youthful teasing. *Mistress...*

What would it be like to be whisked off by a man like Max, ensconced in luxury, cosseted, cared for, indulged...

And held...

There was the crux of the matter. The sweet but poisonous hub.

To be held by such a man. To feel her body sink into his. To be cherished...

'Oh, for heaven's sake, go buy yourself a romance novel,' she muttered. 'Meanwhile, think of this proposition sensibly. It's a business proposal. There's nothing personal about it.'

Phoebe had settled. She was sleeping, a tiny warm being cradled against her breast. That was a siren song too. Babies...

Stop it, stop it, stop it. She gave herself a hard mental shake and turned her feet to home.

And Max was striding towards her in the dusk. Max.

'Stop it,' she muttered again, because her heart was starting to race and it had no business racing. She had to be sensible.

'I'm heading home,' she managed. 'There was no need...'

'There was a need.' He smiled and, oh, that smile...

Stop it!

'You should have told me,' he said reprovingly. 'She's my responsibility. You agreed to help me, not take over entirely.'

'I needed a walk to clear my head.'

'While you think about New York?'

'I can't think about New York. The idea's crazy. We've given you two days board and lodging. You don't need to repay us with the world.'

'Like with like,' he told her. 'You made Phoebe's Mr Sock.'

'Yes, but...'

'And it took you, what, an hour? Plus the thought that went into it beforehand. Tomorrow I'll ring up my father's favoured lawyer. He's a Queen's Counsel. Have you any idea how much such a man demands as an hourly rate?'

'What's that got to do with me?' She tried to walk past him but he put his hand on her arm and stopped her.

'Sunny, value yourself,' he said urgently, 'Give yourself a treat. Believe me when I tell you it'll cost me so little I won't notice.'

And she gazed up at him and realised it really did mean nothing. Handing over first class air tickets, a credit card with no limit, a month in New York for a cleaning lady...

Her thoughts were racing.

Nothing.

Phoebe stirred in her arms and she thought of how easily had Max accepted her. There'd been initial panic but now... He was doing the right thing. He'd take his half-sister back to New York. He'd take Sunny with him to make the transition as easy as possible. Then he'd install a nanny and life would resume its rightful pattern.

He'd be nice to his little sister, she decided, because she'd figured that was what Max was. Nice. Honourable even. He'd do the right thing.

But this man's reputation had come before him. He was an international businessman with fingers in a thousand financial pies. Max had kept below the radar of most of the gossip columnists but the fact that the hotel management bowed and scraped told its own story, and there was enough interest in him to know he was solitary. Aloof.

So yes, he'd care for Phoebe—but would he notice? Would he still walk alone?

She glanced down at Phoebe, at this tiny face still wrinkled from birth. She thought of Phoebe's appalling mother.

And then she thought of her own family, her brothers and sisters, and the fight she'd had to keep them close.

Who would love Phoebe?

Who would fight for Phoebe?

And suddenly the money didn't make sense, the first class flights, the month in New York, the limitless credit card. What made sense was this little life she was holding.

He was still holding her arm. Pressuring her?

Two could play at that game. She tilted her chin and met his gaze full-on.

'Okay,' she said. 'I accept. On one condition.'

'Which is?' He sounded bemused, as well he might. How many women in her place would have imposed a condition? But this was her only chance.

No, it was Phoebe's only chance.

'I'll do it if you take the month off.'

His brows snapped together. 'Sorry?'

'The month I'm there. Yes, I'll come and yes, I'll care for Phoebe. But this housekeeper you say will babysit while I spend your credit card... Does she like babies? Is she kind?'

'I have no idea,' he said honestly. 'But if that doesn't work we can hire...'

'We can't hire,' she said flatly. 'That's the condition. That I come and help, but for the next month her main carer is you. I understand you'll need to do some work but there are home computers and telephones and I'll be in the background. As far as I can see, you're the only person who can possibly learn to love her, so that's what I'm demanding. That you care. I won't stand back and watch as you hand responsibility over to people you hire, at least not until you've figured whether you can love her or not. So there's my line in the sand. We both care for your baby for a month or I don't come. Take it or leave it, Max Grayland, but that's my final word.'

There was a long silence. A very long silence.

Max's hand was still on her arm. They seemed linked in a way she didn't understand, but she needed to focus.

What sort of idiot imposed conditions when faced with such an incredible offer? Max's face said it all. He looked stunned. Incredulous. Was there also the beginnings of anger?

'You think I won't look after her?' he demanded at last and she shook her head.

'You've just proved that you'll look after her with every cent your fortune can provide. But will you love her?'

'She's nothing to do with me,' he snapped. 'She's my father's child.' And yet he paused as if he realised what he'd said. *My father's child.* Family?

'She's a person,' Sunny said, knowing what was at stake here. 'If you intend taking responsibility for her, then surely your life should change. You think you can buy her care? From the sound of things, that's what happened to you. Is that what you want for Phoebe?'

'What happened to me has nothing to do with anything.' It was practically an explosion.

'Doesn't it? Did you have Christmases like we have? How many people would you break your heart over, Max Grayland? I watched you as you struggled to think of your dad's eulogy and I thought I've never seen someone so alone in my life. Is that what you want for Phoebe?'

'No. But I can't take a month off.'

'Really? How many new parents don't take any time off to learn to love their little one? You've just had a new baby. You need to accept it.'

'She's not my baby. And this is…'

'None of my business,' she retorted. 'No, it's not.' She took a deep breath and stepped back from his touch, from his anger, from his pressure. And then she made a decision.

She stepped forward again and, before he knew what she intended, she'd folded Phoebe into his arms. She simply pressed the baby to his chest, waited until his arms closed involuntarily on the sleeping bundle, and then she stepped back.

'If she's not your baby then you need to accept it now,' she told him. 'Buying me won't help you, and it won't help Phoebe. Thank you for the gift, but you need to face it. It was a cop-out for you, and for Phoebe's sake I can't let you take it. The kids will be disappointed. Gran and Pa will be disappointed too, because they'd love to see me travel, but that's the problem with surprise gifts. They have consequences and I can't let those consequences get in the way of Phoebe's care. Take Phoebe back to the house now, Max. I'll be home soon. I just need to walk off a bit of steam.'

She cast him one last look. She saw anger, confusion, shock, but there was nothing she could do about it. Before he could respond she turned away and started walking.

Fast.

For a long moment he didn't move.

He felt as if he was stranded, stuck in time, standing in the dark in a strange country, with a sleeping baby in his arms. He had no idea where Sunny had gone. He couldn't go after her. He had no choice but to turn and walk back to the house.

It was almost surreal, walking under the trees where the nesting parrots stirred and twittered as he passed, where the only lights were those of the muted Christmas decorations in the front yards, where echoes of Christmas music wafted from households readying for bed, readying to farewell Christmas for another year.

Phoebe stayed sleeping in his arms, a warm, fed bundle, nestled against his chest.

You think you can buy her care? Is that what you want for Phoebe?

Sunny's words echoed in his head. He thought of the Christmases he'd had as a child—fantastic, extravagant parties where he was expected to behave, be silent, be grateful and be a charming child for his parents' guests. For there were always guests. They were people he didn't know, the children of his parents' latest lover, business acquaintances, a gathering of society's finest, all trying their darnedest to impress.

He thought of the gifts he'd been given, motorised toy cars—a toy Lamborghini, for heaven's sake—an exquisitely carved rocking horse, designer clothes, vouchers for exclusive stores, sound systems to take his breath away.

And then there'd been the pup.

He'd been eight years old, flown as an unaccompanied minor from the US to England, from boarding school and his father's apartment on the odd weekend to the English country house of his mother's latest lover. Who had a title his mother lusted after. Who welcomed him with affable friendliness. Who bred Border collies.

He could still feel the shock, the joy and the wonder of that Christmas morning. A tiny bundle of black and white fur, moist, licking, wriggling with excitement, with a huge crimson bow around her neck.

'Of course you can keep her. Happy Christmas, darling.'

And he'd fallen completely, besottedly in love.

He'd had her for two months. He'd called her Lassie—how naff was that? but she was the best Christmas gift ever. She'd played with him, exploring the strange farm he'd ended up on. She'd rolled in sheep dung or whatever else disgusting they could find on their adventures. She'd crawled all over him, slept with him, loved him back, a warm, fun bundle of pup he'd thought was his for ever.

But that was the last time he'd ever let himself love. As his mother's relationship folded, as the pretence of happy families disappeared as it always did, he was sent back to his father. That last awful morning…his mother had wrenched the pup from his arms and slapped him when he'd tried to grab her back.

He still couldn't come to terms with the pain of that moment.

He'd do better with Phoebe, he thought. Maybe she could even have a dog? But as he looked down into her sleeping face Sunny's words kept echoing.

You think you can buy her care?

He did think that. This baby had been thrust on him and he had no intention of changing his life. She'd have to fit around the edges.

And, as if on cue, Phoebe opened her eyes and gazed up at him.

Okay, he'd care, he conceded.

But enough to take a month out of his life?

It was more than that, though.

Could he care enough to let himself fall for this tiny creature? Enough to truly acknowledge she was his sister?

There'd been judgement in Sunny's tone and maybe he deserved it. If Phoebe was adopted, if he decided he couldn't care and Isabelle wouldn't, then one of hundreds of couples desperate to have a baby would welcome her with joy. He knew that. They'd certainly take time out of their lives to learn to love her.

They'd open their hearts…

And that was the crux. Opening his heart…

He didn't know how to any more. He was a loner. The lessons learned from his childhood were soul-deep.

So put her up for adoption.

But he gazed down into her face and Sunny's words kept playing and replaying. And then he thought of Sunny's Mr Sock.

'She'd care,' he told Phoebe. And then he added a rider. 'Maybe she can teach me how.'

A month. A month with Phoebe and Sunny.

He thought of the business negotiations waiting for him to deal with as soon as he got back to the States. He thought of complication after complication.

He looked down at Phoebe again and then he thought of Sunny, venting her frustration by walking too fast into the night. He thought of her last night, weary beyond belief, staying up even later to make a Mr Sock.

'Maybe she can teach me,' he said again to Phoebe. But there was something there that… scared him?

Was it Sunny herself? Sunny, with her huge heart. Sunny, with a background so much harder than his, a cleaning lady who sweated blood to love her family.

She deserved her time in New York. She deserved what he could give her.

'So I need to agree to her terms,' he told Phoebe and he thought suddenly of a month in New York with no business. And Sunny.

Surely the sky wouldn't fall on his head if he had a break.

But then… Sunny?

The sky was suddenly threatening and he wasn't sure why.

The way he felt…

You can cut that out, he told himself fiercely as he turned and headed for home. *It's all very well to let yourself fall for a baby. But Sunny?*

Her life was as far from his as it was possible to get.

A month, he told himself. A month and then his life would get back to what it should be.

She walked for an hour, trying to figure what she was doing rejecting such an amazing offer—and also trying to suppress her anger that he'd put such a deal in front of her, a temptation she could almost taste.

She remembered all that time ago, a social worker taking her aside. *'You're a clever girl, Sunny, and the responsibilities you're facing are too much. We'll take you all into care. You can go to school, do what normal kids do, look after Sunny for a change.'*

The social workers had been called in because her mother had been arrested for being drunk and disorderly. They'd found Sunny trying to cope and had been horrified.

Overwhelmed, Sunny had felt herself tempted. To walk away... To have time for Sunny...

It had been a siren song but she'd looked at her brothers and sisters and known there was only one path to tread. She'd reacted with anger; she'd insisted they were all safe and that this episode with her mother had been a one-off. She'd had no choice.

As there was no choice now, but this time it was about Phoebe. 'And she's just as important as Daisy and Sam and Chloe and Tom,' she muttered.

But he'd just employ someone else. Why shouldn't it be her?

'Because I won't watch while he pays me to keep her.' She hiked some more, stomping out her anger.

But she had to go home. With Max's preposterous suggestion off the table she needed to go to work tomorrow. It was almost midnight. She needed to sleep.

As if that was going to happen. But she turned and made her reluctant way home, trying not to think of New York. Trying not to think of Phoebe.

Trying not to think of Max.

She turned into the driveway and Max was sitting on the veranda steps. Waiting.

'Hi.'

For some reason she wanted to turn and run but she forced herself to keep walking. His greeting was low and gravelly. The rest of the house must be asleep—the house was in darkness. The window behind him into the room he shared with Phoebe was open but there was silence there as well. He'd have put her down and come outside—to wait for her?

'Hi,' she managed and headed for the steps. She needed to brush past fast. 'G…goodnight. I need to go to bed.'

'I need you to come to New York.'

'I already told you…' She was halfway up the stairs, trying to brush past him fast.

'Of your conditions. I accept.'

She stopped dead. Her world seemed to wobble and she had to put out a hand on the balustrade to steady herself.

'Really?' she managed.

'Really. And Sunny, I'm sorry.'

'For…for what?'

'For not getting it.' He edged aside. 'Will you sit down?'

'I need…'

'To listen. Oh, and I have the brandy sauce.'

'You…what?'

'Ruby was up making herself a cup of tea and eating a mince pie when I got home. She diluted some of the brandy sauce into a jug, with orders to give you some. And she told me to tell you to quit it with the qualms, take my offer and run.'

She smiled, despite her…qualms. 'That sounds like Gran.'

He poured two glasses and held one out. 'Sit,' he told her.

She should… She should…

She sat.

'So, about this offer,' Max said. 'It's still open. A month in New York, all expenses paid; the only catch is now you'll need to put up with me a bit more than you expected.'

Yeah, that'd be a disaster, she thought, but she didn't say it. How inappropriate was that?

'So you'll take a month off work?' she managed. She needed to get this clear. She needed to get a lot of things clear.

'Mostly.' He gave a rueful smile. 'There'll be things I need to attend to. Dad's death has left loose ends that need to be tied but, as you say, I have a computer and a phone. Everything that can be put off will be put off.'

'For Phoebe.'

'For Phoebe.' He handed her the glass and clinked his. 'So is this to shared childminding?'

'I… I guess.' She was too hornswoggled to

make much sense. She tipped the glass…and practically choked. 'What the…?'

He drank too, and grinned. 'I guess she diluted it with more brandy, huh?'

'My grandmother…' She glowered and he grinned and it broke the tension.

'She's awesome.'

'She is,' Sunny agreed. This was a safe topic at least. 'I don't know that I can leave her.'

'If there weren't others to care I'd say not. But you know you can.'

'If anything happened to Pa…'

'I'd have you on the next plane. But Daisy tells me it's not likely.'

'Did she tell you about his heart?'

'He has a new stent. It seems to be working. Daisy says there are no promises but he's better now than he has been. She also says this might be your only window before…before something does happen.'

'A window…'

'A window to do something different, something that might even be fun. Something for Sunny. Your whole family wants this for you, Sunny. So just say yes.'

'My whole family and you.'

'That's right.'

'Why?' She took another sip of her brandy sauce and then carefully set it down. Who knew what strength it was, and she needed every bit of concentration she could muster. 'New York will be full of extraordinary childminders, nannies, the works. Americans don't take January off. You could employ someone in a flash.'

'And I'm good at employing people,' he agreed. 'I could find someone highly skilled, great work ethic, honest, capable, efficient. But I'm not sure if that's what Phoebe needs. I run a huge corporation, Sunny, and I've learned others have the skills I don't. Hiring nannies… I don't have the first clue. All I know is that I want someone like you. I know you can't take the job permanently, but if you give me a month we can find someone together.'

How did she answer that?

So why not?

Max was throwing money at her problems. Chloe and Tom were more than capable of taking care of Gran and Pa, and they'd love the chance to stay here rather than take the menial holiday jobs they had to do to survive. Gran and Pa would love their company, love the extra attention. Daisy and Sam would be in the background, ready to help.

Max had somehow wangled her leave without pay. She could return in a month and walk back into her job.

So why not?

Because…because…

He was too close.

And there was the reason in a nutshell. She was sitting beside him in the dark. The step wasn't wide enough to allow any distance. His body was brushing against hers.

She could feel his heat. She could sense his strength.

It made her feel…frightened?

Not exactly. It was a sensation she had no way of describing.

Oh, for heaven's sake… She was quibbling and why? She knew this man was honourable—the fact that he'd come here with his baby rather than taking Phoebe to the nearest welfare worker told her that. His name was known the world over. If there was any of…what Gran would call 'funny business'…she could have his name plastered over every tabloid in the Western world.

'You can trust me,' he said and infuriatingly there was laughter behind his words. How did he know? 'Huge apartment,' he continued. 'Master bedroom one end. Guest suite at the other with about an acre of living room in between.'

'It sounds…lonely,' she managed.

'Lonely's the way I like it. But with Phoebe… I guess I need to change. I'm depending on you to teach me.'

'Lonely's never been a problem for me,' she managed. 'Sometimes I…'

'Wouldn't mind a taste? This is your chance.

I promise I'll do as much of the caring as I can. You'll have time to yourself. Real time. I'm guessing for you that could be worth gold.'

'I…yes.' But she wasn't sure.

'So you'll come?'

She looked at him in the moonlight, a big, solitary man she knew nothing of apart from his reputation as one of the world's most ruthless businessmen.

But she did know him better than that, she thought. She'd watched the way he held Phoebe. She'd seen the pain as he'd fought for something to say at his father's funeral. She'd watched him lose himself in the kids' silly basketball match and she'd listened to him talk to Pa. Pa was a bit forgetful, a bit inclined to tell the same stories over and over, but Max had listened with courtesy and interest. He'd made Pa smile.

And what he was offering…

Just say yes.

'Yes,' she said and it felt as if she'd just jumped off a very high cliff.

What had she done?

But Max was setting his glass down and turning to face her. He took her hands in his and it felt right. It felt…as if the world was slowing down to let something important happen. Something out of her control?

'Thank you,' he said and she found her breathing wasn't quite happening. But who needed to breathe when the world was tipping on its axis?

What was in that brandy sauce?

'I think…' How to get her voice above a whisper? 'I think it's the wrong way around. It's me who should be thanking you. This is…an extraordinary offer.'

'You deserve it. You're an extraordinary woman.'

'I'm a cleaning lady.'

'And so much more. Don't you dare devalue yourself. Has anyone ever told you how beautiful you are?'

She practically laughed. Beautiful? With her worn hands, her hair she cut herself, her faded clothes… He had to be mocking.

But his eyes weren't mocking. His eyes said he spoke the truth and for one glorious moment she let herself believe. For this wasn't her. This was some other woman, sitting in the moonlight with the most beautiful man…

This was a tableau, make-believe, magic.

But she couldn't make it stop, and why would she? For he was drawing her gently to him. No pressure. She could pull away at any moment. She could…

She couldn't, for he'd released one of her hands, and with his free hand he was tilting her chin. He was cupping her face. He was tilting her mouth to his.

And kissing…

She'd been kissed before—of course she had. She knew how kissing could feel.

Only it wasn't like this.

It was as if her body simply fused. His hands caught her waist and he tugged her close. The moment their mouths met… The sensations… The heat, the strength, the feel of him… The taste… The sheer masculine scent…

The rasp of after-five shadow. The strength of his jawline. The tenderness with strength and urgency behind it.

She was sinking into him, melting, aching to be a part of something she had no hope of understanding. Did she whimper? She hoped not but she might have. She'd never felt like this. She was sitting on her grandparents' front step and yet she felt a world away, transported into another life. A life where there was just Max and Sunny.

Fantasy.

And with that thought reality came slamming in, like a wash of ice water. What was she doing? She, Sunny, was sitting on the porch kissing a billionaire, a man who'd just employed her, a man who was about to be her boss.

And Chloe's words were suddenly right there. *'She mightn't mind being his mistress.'*

What sort of dangerous game was this?

Somehow she managed to tug away. She was

released in an instant. She sat staring at him and thought... *He looks almost as stunned as me.*

'No,' she stammered.

'No?'

'I...you're employing me. This is...you have no right.'

'I don't.' But he sounded regretful.

'It won't work if you...if you take liberties.'

And the ready laughter flashed back. 'Liberties? If I'm not mistaken, you were kissing back.'

She couldn't deny it. Nor did she want to, but some things had to be set straight.

'Enough.' She rose and brushed her hands on her jeans as if wiping away a stain. 'That was an aberration.'

'There's a big word.'

A big word. Whoa?

And reality slammed right back, as it always did. She was the dumb one, the kid who'd hardly been to school, the one who'd been lucky to get a job as a hotel cleaner. What right did she have to use big words?

What right did she have to kiss this guy and, if she did, what would he expect in return?

'Yeah, I must have read it on the back of a cornflakes packet,' she muttered. 'Aberration. Deviation from the norm. Beware, there's the odd cornflake in here that might not meet expectations. Just like me saying aberration.'

'I'm sorry.' He got her anger. 'Sunny, I didn't mean…' He started to rise but she backed away.

'I accept your offer of a job,' she told him. 'My family's right; it's an awesome offer too good to refuse. And I'll do my best. I'll care for Phoebe as I'd care for my own family, but that's all I'm committing to. I'm staff, Max Grayland, the hired help, so don't you dare try anything on with me.'

'I wouldn't…'

'You just did.'

'Wasn't it consensual?'

'There's another big word,' she snapped. 'That's beside the point. I'm the hired help, got it? Stay clear of me, Max Grayland. I'll work for you, I'll care for Phoebe and I'll probably enjoy it, but if you touch me again I'll tell you where you can put your consensual. Now, goodnight. Christmas is over and I'm done. Oh, and I'll do Phoebe's next feed. I'm paid staff, remember, and I start being treated as paid staff right now.'

Paid staff

He'd kissed her and she didn't feel like paid staff at all.

He had no idea what she felt like. He tried to analyse it and all he could come up with was… different. The bland adjective didn't begin to describe his reaction.

No one like Sunny had ever come into his orbit.

She was a hotel cleaner and yet she wasn't. Or she was, but she was so much more. He was seeing beneath the outer layer but there were more layers concealing what lay underneath, complexities he had no way of knowing.

Did he want to know?

He didn't. Of course he didn't, because he had no wish to become involved.

Forty-eight hours ago a baby had been thrust into his life, making him more involved than he'd ever wanted to be. Threatening his precious independence. And here was Sunny...threatening the same?

Except she wasn't. Sunny knew the rules.

'I'm paid staff, remember, and I start being treated as paid staff right now.'

So what was he doing, kissing her? He'd pushed hard to get her to come to New York. It was a sensible plan to solve his problems, not a first step in making more.

Kissing her made more.

No. Feeling as he did made more. The touch of her...the taste of her lips...the warmth of her body...the twinkle, the strength, the love...

Love. There was a scary word. She had it in abundance, he thought—love to share.

He wanted it for Phoebe so he was paying for it, but he didn't want it for himself. He knew the perils of loving and he had no intention of going there. Kissing Sunny had risked his perfectly crafted plans for nothing.

'So keep your hands to yourself.' He said it out loud and then noticed the open window and wondered if Sunny was inside—if Sunny could hear.

So what? Let her think what had happened was simply a *boss makes an inappropriate move* moment. He'd apologise in the morning, trust she didn't sue for sexist harassment in the workplace and move on.

But the way the kiss had made him feel…

'Move on,' he told himself, again out loud, roughly, harshly. 'You have enough complications without that.'

'Oi!' The voice above his head startled him. It was Tom, leaning out of an upstairs window. 'Are you enjoying talking to yourself or would you like company?'

'Thanks but no.' He rose and walked down the steps so he could grin ruefully up at Tom. 'Sorry to disturb you.'

'You sure you don't want a mate to drink with?'

'Thank you but no. I'm heading to bed and I'm happy on my own.'

'People who talk to themselves aren't happy on their own,' Tom said sagely. 'Just lucky our Sunny's going back to New York with you.'

'Yes, it is,' he agreed and headed inside.

But should he have agreed? His head—and his body—were starting to have all sorts of doubts.

Was it lucky that Sunny was coming back with him?

It was sensible, he told himself. But it also felt…

Risky.

CHAPTER EIGHT

THE FLIGHT TO New York was awesome, though it might just ruin her for flying for ever. How could she ever appreciate cattle class now? Her first ever time in an aeroplane was a first class flight, with extra seats booked for Phoebe and her baby gear.

Max Grayland was obviously a platinum flyer, privileged beyond belief. Every time he blinked— or Sunny blinked—someone was there to help. Who knew what the flight attendants thought of her, but not by a twitch of their perfectly groomed faces did they show how out of place her faded jeans and discount store jacket looked in this place.

For the most part Max stayed engrossed in his work. It was urgent stuff, she gathered, by the way his fingers flew over the keyboard and by the amount of paperwork littered around his seat. But he was taking her stipulation seriously. When Phoebe was awake he'd leave his work and take the baby from her. He'd dandle her and smile and play, and Sunny watched him and thought she was almost redundant.

Except…she was included too. They had four seats, two pairs across the aisle from each other. When Phoebe was awake Max moved to the seat next to hers. He chatted to his little sister, he told her all the treats that were in store for her in New York, but he included Sunny in the conversation.

'It'll be cold,' he told his little sister. 'Really cold. That's the first thing we need to do, get you some warm baby clothes. And Sunny too. A decent down jacket, I think, and some fur-lined boots so you two can explore together.'

'I can...' Sunny started but she knew she couldn't. She didn't have the wherewithal to buy her own down jacket and she'd have no clue as to where to buy a cheap one.

'You probably could,' Max agreed gravely, giving her her dignity. 'But it would be my privilege to buy them for you. Besides, girls like shopping and it'll be fun watching you two hit the stores.'

'Fun?' She didn't believe him.

'Okay, I have no idea if it'll be fun,' he admitted. 'But grant me the privilege of finding out.'

And then they were landing. A chauffeur met them and a limousine took them straight to Max's apartment. She had a brief impression of a vast park on one side of the street, with old stone buildings on the other, solid and imposing. Then they were ushered inside and Sunny could barely take in such luxury. A housekeeper with a smiley face and a head full of tight white curls greeted them with pleasure.

'Supper or bed?' Max asked Sunny, and the care and empathy in his smile was almost her undoing.

For despite the luxury, despite the attention—or maybe because of it, because it had left her in a limbo of tension as she'd tried to figure what her role was—she was exhausted.

'I…just a cup of tea and bed,' she told him. 'But I'll settle Phoebe…'

'How about a toasted cheese sandwich and cocoa in bed?' Max asked. 'Eliza and I can look after Phoebe, can't we, Eliza?'

And Eliza was nodding and smiling, scooping Phoebe out of her carry capsule and cradling her with care. Making Phoebe even less sure of her role.

'We certainly can. I'll show you to your bedroom, Miss Raye. May I suggest a bath—a nice long soak—and then supper and bed?' And she smiled at Max and she smiled down at Phoebe. 'Oh, Mr Grayland, this is going to be fun.'

So she lay in a king-sized tub with bubbles up to her neck and tried to figure what was going on. She was ensconced in luxury and Max Grayland had a housekeeper who looked like everyone's favourite granny.

How could she be needed? Phoebe was just one little girl…

Who was wailing. Maybe she'd been in the bath a tad long. Maybe she'd almost snoozed. She dried fast and wrapped a bathrobe round her—hey, Max had those fancy hotel-type robes, only better. She wrapped her wet hair in one of his gorgeous towels and padded out to see.

Max was pacing the floor with Phoebe, encouraging her to take the bottle. Phoebe, however, was having none of it.

For a moment she stood in the doorway and watched him. The living room was enormous, with vast plate glass windows showing the skyline of practically all of Manhattan. The room itself was amazing, luxury meshed with indescribable comfort. It was a living room with a kitchen/dining area. There were vast planked benches, a polished wood floor with tapestry rugs, sofas and chairs you'd just want to sink into, a planked table that matched the benches with twelve leather chairs, a fireplace with a crackling fire augmenting the obviously very efficient central heating...

And a man who couldn't handle a baby.

'Drink it, sweetheart.' He was almost pleading. 'We need to show Sunny we can cope.'

His hair was ruffled, his shirt was half out and he looked...baffled? He was a man in unfamiliar territory. But he lived here, she reminded herself before taking pity on him.

'Do you need help?'

His expression of almost pathetic gratitude made her laugh. 'Yes. Please.'

'Hey, it's not that bad.'

'She says it is.'

'Where's Eliza?'

'She finished at seven. She comes in for an hour in the morning and then for a couple of hours in the evening. She makes me supper and leaves it in the warming drawer. Which reminds me, your toasted cheese sandwich is in the oven.'

'I'll have it later.' She scooped Phoebe out of Max's arms and cradled her against her breast, gently rocking. 'Hey, sweetheart. Hey, little one.'

Max proffered the bottle but she shook her head. 'She won't take it like this. I need to calm her down first.' She kept on rocking and crooning while she looked out of the window at the truly amazing view and thought that this man had everything...

Everything? A housekeeper who leaves his supper in the warming drawer?

'Eliza seems lovely,' she said, while Phoebe hiccupped life's tragedies into her shoulder. 'Surely she could help you look after Phoebe.'

'I wouldn't know.'

'How do you mean? She seems caring.'

'I've only met her twice.' Max sounded almost goaded. 'I met her when I hired her and gave her the key to the apartment. Her references were great, her cooking's excellent and she cleans efficiently. That's hardly enough of a reference to leave Phoebe with her, even if I knew she had time to spare. I know nothing about her personal life.'

'But if you did?' Privately she felt okay that he

had qualms. He wouldn't leave Phoebe with just anyone, but instinct told her Eliza was solid. 'You could check her out and I could go home now.'

'Do you want to?'

Well, there was a question.

She'd seen the bed she'd be sleeping in. It was the king of plush, luxurious beyond measure. Outside the windows of this magnificent apartment stretched all of Manhattan. Of course she didn't want to go home.

But it was more than that.

Max was standing by the window, seemingly as exhausted as she was, and suddenly she thought… *He seems alone.*

It was a weird thing to think. This man had the world at his feet. The Grayland Corporation employed thousands worldwide. He could snap his fingers and have a dozen employees here to take care of Phoebe right now.

But… His housekeeper came in while he was at work, made him dinner and left it in the warming drawer and he didn't know her. This place was designer perfect but, glancing around, she saw no signs of personality. There were no photographs, no silly souvenirs or fridge magnets. She thought of the jumble of detritus in her grandparents' house and she thought…

Maybe she *was* lucky?

The thought came from out of left field, so unexpected that it almost blindsided her. For the past few years—okay, maybe for all her life—she'd existed by doing what came next. The arrival of her grandparents on the scene had seemed a miracle. The worst of the threats had disappeared and she'd been loved and protected ever since. But it hadn't stopped the grind of daily life. Ruby and John were living in a tumbledown home they didn't own. They had life tenure so they couldn't sell it, and there was no way they could afford to rent a home that'd be big enough for all of them. Their daughter had robbed them blind and put them deep in debt during her early drug-taking years and they had no money, so Sunny was forced to keep on working, putting one foot in front of the other as she did what she'd sworn to do. She'd get her siblings an education. She'd see them safe.

But she'd missed out herself. Apart from the blessings of having Gran and Pa on the scene, she'd never once thought she was lucky.

But now, standing in this grand apartment, looking at this man standing solitary against windows overlooking the world, she thought maybe she was.

And she thought…a month. Maybe in a month she could show him…fun. In her arms she held the embryo of a family. Max's family. With luck Phoebe could grow to be a bouncy, happy toddler, a cheerful little girl, a child who'd greet her big brother with joy when he got home every night. He could be a big brother who'd collect her from school, who'd attend interminable school concerts, who'd commiserate over broken love affairs and bad hairstyles.

He didn't have a clue, she thought, and she had a month to teach him.

Phoebe had settled to the stage where her sobs were simply hiccups of exhaustion. Sunny sank onto one of the massive down-filled armchairs and held her hand out for the bottle. Max handed it to her and then perched on the chair's wide arm and watched while Phoebe fed.

'You make it seem easy.'

'I make it seem like I've done this before.'

'For all your siblings?'

'As far as I remember. I was only five when Daisy was born so Mum must have been around, but I still remember making bottles in the middle of the night.'

'Hell, Sunny…'

'I loved them,' she said simply. 'It's easy when you love. I learned that early.' She smiled down into Phoebe's face, now tightly screwed up in concentration as she sucked. 'I'd take Daisy into bed with me and cuddle her and we'd go back to sleep together. She was better than a doll.'

And it was *much* better than being alone. She remembered that too, the sound of the door slamming as her mother left for the night, and the warmth of the baby in her arms. She'd been something to hold onto.

What did Max hold onto?

He was right by her. His hip was brushing against her arm. She could…

She couldn't.

'So what shall we do tomorrow?' she asked, forcing a brightness she didn't feel.

'Sleep?'

'Will you sleep?'

'Probably not. I'm used to crossing time zones. But I'll work from home while you catch up on Zs. I won't wake you unless I need you.'

'Wake me anyway. I'm only here for a month and I don't want to miss a minute. Besides, two people giving cuddles are much better than one.'

There was a moment's silence. He was looking down at her and the feeling was…weird? She glanced up at him and then looked away.

She didn't understand what was happening. She'd never felt like this and it frightened her, but the look on his face said he was almost as confounded as she was.

'Let's take tomorrow as it comes,' he said. 'It's Saturday. Eliza won't be here so I may well need you.'

'I hope you do.' But then she thought should she have said that?

She was in unknown territory and she didn't have a clue where to take it.

Take it to bed, she thought. Bed was good. Time out, in her gorgeous bedroom.

Phoebe had finished her bottle. She hoisted her onto her shoulder and rubbed her back and was rewarded with a satisfactory burp. 'You have somewhere for this little one to sleep?'

'I had Eliza organise it.' He rose and she followed, carrying the sleeping Phoebe. He opened the bedroom door next to hers and it was all she could do not to gasp.

Okay, she did gasp. It was an ode to pink and silver, a baby's nursery like no other. The wallpaper was embossed with pink and silver elephants. Pink curtains covered the windows and lush pink carpet covered the floor. A magnificent cot stood at one end, white and silver with pink bedding. There was a pram that looked like something Mary Poppins would push, a true English perambulator. A baby bath on a stand. A myriad of beautiful mobiles hanging from the ceiling. An open wardrobe full of pink.

'What…how did this happen?' she gasped.

'My staff had notice. You can buy anything with money.'

She stared around her in astonishment while Max lifted the sleeping Phoebe from her arms and laid her in her cot.

'See? No cushions and a nice firm mattress,' he told her. 'But a buffer to stop her hitting the sides. My instructions were explicit.'

'Good for you,' she managed as Phoebe stirred and snuffled and then settled to serious sleep. 'But there's no adjoining door into my room. I won't hear her in the night.'

'That's what this is for.' He held up a state-of-the-art baby monitor. 'But the receiver's in my room. I'm taking this seriously.'

'I…good.'

She had no cause for complaint.

But then as she gazed around the magnificent nursery she found herself thinking of the one-bedroom apartment she'd been raised in, the jumble of kids and noise and chaos, the ancient cane bassinet used by successive babies until they were big enough to join the tangle of kids in the shared bed.

And she looked at Phoebe in her magnificent crib and she looked at the vast room and the state-of-the-art baby monitor, and she looked again at Max, who thought he had it all under control.

But his expression said he wasn't sure. His expression said maybe he had as many doubts as she did—but now wasn't the time for voicing them.

'Goodnight, then,' she told him, and almost before she knew what she intended, she crossed the room and stood on tiptoe and kissed him lightly on the cheek. It was a feather-touch, a brush of friendship. 'You've done good, Max Grayland. Good luck with your baby monitor.'

She was gone, deviating back to the kitchen to grab her sandwich and a glass of milk—a girl had to be practical—then heading to her room and shutting the door behind her.

And there was no reason in the world why Max Grayland stood in the baby's darkened room with his hand to his cheek.

No reason at all.

CHAPTER NINE

TRUE TO HIS WORD, Max kept the baby monitor. On Sunny's first morning in New York she slept until ten, which was almost unheard-of for her. She yelped when she saw the time and bounced out of bed, to find Max at his desk at the far end of the massive living room with Phoebe in her perambulator beside him.

'We took a few rounds of the apartment,' he told her with evident pride. 'She likes the perambulator. She got a bit scratchy for a while and we were worried we'd wake you but it didn't reach full-throated roar. We decided she was just bored. So we went up and down in the elevator a few times and I explained its workings. She was most interested and now she's gone to sleep to dream of counterweights and pulleys. Her eyes glazed over a bit when I started on elevator algorithms but she's young. She'll get it in time.'

'She...you talked elevator algorithms...?'

'She's smart.' Max's voice held all the pride of a new dad. 'She'll have it nailed by this time next week.'

'Of course she will.' She was having trouble keeping her voice steady.

'Breakfast? I'm up for a second. Waffles? We

have a waffle maker and Eliza's made up a batter. Eggs? Bacon? Maple syrup? You name it.' And then he looked at her more closely. 'And then back to bed, I think. The weather's filthy, wind blowing straight from the Arctic. Phoebe and I are doing fine.'

'I can't… I'm here to work.'

'You're here as backup,' he said, seriously now. 'That was the deal. And Sunny, you can't tell me you don't need a break. The alcove over there is my library. We have movies to stream, newspapers, video games… There's a lap pool in the basement and a gym. Anything you want…'

'I didn't come for a holiday.'

'No,' he agreed. 'You came to give me the courage to do what I'm doing, and you're succeeding.' He was smiling, his eyes kind but also…searching? As if he could see the bone-deep weariness that had been with her almost since she was born. 'So while you're succeeding, how about looking after Sunny for a change?' He rose. 'Okay, you're about to see a sight that's not been seen by many. Max Grayland cooking.'

'Can you?'

'I think so,' he said and grinned. 'Eliza's left me instructions. How hard can one waffle be?'

The waffle was excellent but it was hard to concentrate. Sunny ate in silence. She drank juice and coffee. She looked out of the windows at the vision of a rain-soaked Central Park. She tried not to look at Max.

How could she stay here for four weeks…so close…when he just had to smile…?

But as she finished her coffee he excused himself and headed back to his desk, and Phoebe.

'If you'll pardon us, we have work to do,' he told Sunny. 'Bed again? Or whatever you like. Your choice.'

Sunny glanced at the gleaming dishwasher and thought she didn't even have to wash a mug. She had time to herself… The sensation was so extraordinary she felt as if she were floating.

She wouldn't mind…just sitting and watching Max with Phoebe.

He was back at his desk, sorting papers but glancing occasionally at the sleeping baby by his side. He looked tense, but he was trying. He was taking this seriously.

He wanted a little sister?

The vision of Phoebe's over-the-top nursery was suddenly front and centre and she didn't need to be told that this was how Max had been raised. A loner. A guy who didn't do family.

But he was trying and she'd been sent back to bed.

As if she could sleep. *Ha!* But to go back to bed…to have nothing to do…

She edged towards the library and Max cast her a glance of approval. 'Anything you like…'

Anything she liked. There was a concept that had the power to disconcert her all by itself. But she checked the books and saw what was there and almost forgot Max and Phoebe.

Five minutes later she was scuttling back to her bedroom, clutching an armload of tomes.

A whole day. Books. Warmth. Bed...

And Max Grayland sitting in the room next door, gently rocking his baby sister.

They spent the weekend ensconced in their cocoon while Max figured Phoebe out and Sunny tried to figure herself out. There were times when Phoebe's needs required her attention but Max was trying manfully to cope by himself. His phone was never silent but when Phoebe needed his attention he switched it off. Sunny was starting to feel seriously impressed.

This man had been thrown a baby out of left field and he was doing his best. Sure, there were times when Phoebe screamed and nothing he could do seemed to placate her. That was what babies did and all she could do was reassure him.

'A doctor once told me being a paediatrician's like being a vet,' she told him at two a.m. on the Monday morning when they were taking turns walking the circuit of the living room. 'Babies and dogs...you know when they're miserable but they can't tell you what's wrong.'

'So what's wrong?'

'Who knows?' She adjusted the screaming baby on her shoulder. 'She's not hungry. She's clean and dry and warm. Maybe her tummy's taking time to adjust to formula. Maybe she doesn't like your colour scheme. Maybe she's just figuring how her lungs work.'

'Or maybe she's ill.'

'Maybe she is,' Sunny told him. 'But if you take her to Emergency and tell them she's been screaming for less than an hour they'll grin and say *Welcome to the world of babies*. Chances are the moment you're admitted to see the doctor she'll go to sleep.'

'So I ignore screaming.'

'You cuddle screaming. It's the quiet stuff that's scary.'

'The quiet stuff?' They were talking over Phoebe's sobs and Phoebe's sobs were doing something to him. Making him feel helpless? Making him feel he could never cope alone.

'That's when the doctors jump,' Sunny told him. 'A limp baby who's off her food and doesn't have the energy to cry is a scary thing.'

'Is that what you had to cope with?' If he was frightened of being alone...how much worse would it have been for Sunny?

'I learned the difference. I took Tom to the hospital one night when he wouldn't stop crying but he was fine and next thing I knew we had a bevy of social workers breathing down our necks. They didn't like the idea of a ten-year-old presenting with a sick baby. Mum nearly killed me.'

'But she didn't take him herself?'

'She wasn't home. Hey, I think your sister's asleep. Finally. You want me to take her in with me? Not in my bed,' she said hastily. 'In the pram beside me.'

'What's wrong with her room?'

'It's lonely. Maybe that's why she's crying. Who'd want to be alone?'

And he looked at her oddly.

This was a weird intimacy.

Max was looking absurdly good for a guy woken in the middle of the night, but maybe having a gorgeous haircut, after-five shadow that looked downright sexy and pretty decent blue and white striped pyjamas did that for a guy. Whereas she was wearing a bad haircut and an oversized nightie she'd bought in an op shop two years ago.

'Have you ever been alone?' he asked.

She tilted her head and looked at him, considering. The question, the way he made her feel, the way she was feeling—strangely aware of his vulnerability—made her answer with honesty.

'Alone? Hardly ever,' she told him. 'I'd imagine that's your specialty. But lonely...that night when I was scared for Tom, and all the other nights... you'd better believe it. But since Gran and Pa gave us a home I've pretty much forgotten what lonely feels like and I never want to go back there. So will you let her sleep with me? I swear she won't miss her pink palace.'

'She can sleep with me if you think she needs company.' He was watching her as if he couldn't figure her out. 'Though it'll take some getting used to—not being alone.'

'There are advantages,' she said, forcing herself to sound brisk. Employee chatting to employer. In her nightgown. 'Here's hoping she doesn't snore. I'll head back to bed then. Alone. I kind of like it.'

'Sunny…'

'Mmm?'

'What would you like to do tomorrow? The forecast is reasonable. We could pack Phoebe up and…perambulate. First stop is to buy you a decent jacket and shoes. Next… The Statue of Liberty? The Empire State Building? You name it. Let's go sightseeing.'

'You don't need to work?'

'We made a deal. I'm sticking to it. Besides,' he admitted, 'it might be fun.'

'I bet you've already seen the Statue of Liberty.'

'I have,' he agreed. 'But she's worth a second look.'

'Or a thousandth?'

'Sunny…whatever you want.'

She hesitated. *What she really wanted…*

She thought back to the pile of books she'd been reading and thought, *Why not say it?*

'How about City Hall Station?'

'City Hall Station?' he said blankly. 'What the…?'

'You have influence, right?'

'I…yes.'

'I hoped you might. You'd need to pull a few strings to get us down there but they say there are guides who can organise it. Do you know what I'm talking of?'

'I have no idea.'

'It's not used. I've just been reading about it. It was opened in 1904, deep in the belly of New York's subway system. Apparently it's a beautiful, untouched station that hardly anyone seems to know about. The architecture's amazing. Apart from the skill of the engineering, it has the most gorgeous tiled arches, untouched brass fixtures that take your breath away and magnificent skylights running across the entire curve of the station.'

'Why isn't it used?' he said faintly.

'It was gorgeous but stupid. The engineers got everything right, apart from the biggie. Train carriages are long, neat rectangles, but the tracks at the platform are so curved they couldn't stop the train without leaving a gap between the doors and the platform. Crazy, huh? It was used for a while with restrictions and then closed in 1945. I'd love to see it.'

'But…why?'

And he had her on her hobby horse. Despite the

hour, despite the weirdness of the setting, she told him. 'I love tunnels,' she confessed. 'There was an opening to a drain near us when I was a kid and I used to go exploring. The authorities have wised up to risks now and there are protective barriers in place. There aren't many opportunities to go underground, but then...'

'You went down drains?' he said faintly. 'On your own?'

And she hesitated but then decided. Why not tell him?

'It was my retreat,' she confessed. 'How corny's that? I was always sensible—watchful for weather even when I was very small. But I remember... early on, one of Mum's boyfriends hit me and I ran away. I found the drain, the opening to the tunnel and I sat in it for hours, far in, where no one could find me but I could still see the arch of the opening. Maybe I should have been frightened but the dim light, the silence, the huge, solid stones around me...somehow they made me feel safe. By the time I came out again I felt...stronger.'

'Sunny!'

'Dumb, isn't it,' she said sheepishly. 'It makes no sense but there it is. And it's stayed. Tunnels. I love 'em. The skill in making them... Can you imagine digging underground, then building vast stone arches so they met at the top, strong enough to handle the load of a city, cars, people, buildings, even trains?' She shook her head. 'If I had more education I'd have done engineering and learned how to dig them. I even tried to get a job on a construction crew when I was fifteen, but apparently teenage girls aren't what they want around hard hats and diggers. But I read about them and now... The City Hall station... I bet you could get me down there.'

'Maybe,' he said cautiously. 'If I chose...'

'So will you choose?'

'Phoebe...'

'It's not dangerous. If we're buying me a coat we could also buy a baby cocoon. Then Phoebe can see City Hall Station too. I bet that's why she's been crying. I was telling her about it this afternoon and she thought she'd miss out. But wouldn't that be a cool thing to do?'

'I...very cool.' Wandering through unused underground subway stations instead of doing the work that was piling up...

But Sunny was looking at him with eyes that were bright with excitement. She'd woken at two in the morning to help him with a screaming baby. She was wearing a nightgown that was too big, faded, frayed around the hem. Her hair was tousled, she was wearing no make-up, there was a smattering of freckles on the bridge of her nose...

He had the strongest desire to kiss...

Um...not. She was holding his baby.

Not his baby.

His world was feeling more and more lopsided.

'Do you still want to dig tunnels?' he asked faintly and she grinned.

'I've let that go,' she said with regret. 'I imagine tunnelling would require years of hands-on experience and it's too late for that now.' She took a deep breath. 'But I would so love to study architecture. And I will.'

She suddenly seemed to have stars in her eyes, a kid thinking of Christmas. *It's a dream*, he told himself, and he shouldn't mess with dreams. 'That's um…great,' he said weakly. 'Good for you.'

Her twinkle didn't fade but her look became speculative. 'You think I'm nuts.'

'I think…it'll be hard.'

'But not impossible.'

'I guess… What age did you leave school?'

'I hardly went to school, but that doesn't mean I don't know stuff. I pushed every one of my siblings through years of homework. Calculus? Geography? Try me. But universities need proof, so that's what I'm doing. Slowly and online but I'm four university entrance units down. After another two I can apply. The course will take me years because I'll still need to work but by the time I'm forty I might just be there. A fully-fledged architect. How cool would that be?'

'Very cool,' he managed, stunned. He shook his head. 'How many things in your life are cool?'

'Lots. And yours?'

'I...maybe.' But he'd never looked at life with the zest and enthusiasm this woman had. She was blowing him away.

'Bed,' she said now, with the same enthusiasm. 'We have a big day tomorrow and Phoebe might wake up again.'

'She might but she can sleep in my room while she decides.'

She'd taken Phoebe off her shoulder and was cradling her against her breast. Phoebe's face had relaxed in sleep. The screaming jag was done. Sunny was smiling down at her, as peaceful as the baby herself.

He came close to take her, and then paused. Caught by the night. The quiet. The total silence.

This woman who'd been through so much, who'd faced the world with such bravery, who had so much to give...

This woman was beautiful.

She looked up at him, questioning, wondering why he was hesitating. Her face was tilted...

She seemed infinitely precious, infinitely fragile.

He shouldn't. She was alone in his apartment. She was his employee. She was totally vulnerable...

'If you want to kiss me then kiss me,' she said, and suddenly she was grinning.

'What?'

'Have I misread the signs?'

'No.' He was smiling too. 'You haven't. But Sunny... Back in Australia...'

'I know. I stopped you because it seemed scary. You're my employer and there seemed all sorts of minefields. So maybe there are but right now... You know, right now I'm over being sensible. It felt good then and somehow I suspect it might feel even better now.' And then, as she looked at his face, the hint of mischief returned. 'Oh, for heaven's sake, Max Grayland, just kiss me.'

And what was a man to do? He chuckled. And then he kissed her.

The first time Max had kissed her, two weeks ago now, she'd felt as if her world had changed, and, to be honest, there'd been a voice inside her all this time demanding she try again. Was that first reaction her imagination?

It wasn't.

It was as if her breathing had been taken over by another. More, it was as if her body had been taken over. She was no longer Sunny.

Somehow, two parts of a whole, a being she hadn't known existed, had been miraculously brought together and joined. Every piece fitted into place and now its heat was soldering them together in some way that could never be undone.

Weird? Fanciful? She didn't care. All she cared about was that she was in his arms. Phoebe was tucked between them, warm and safe, both of their bodies curved to protect her, and that was weird too. It was as if Phoebe was part of them. A bonding that couldn't be undone?

But these feelings were subliminal, a wash of sensation, a wave of intuition that told her she was right out of her comfort zone but somehow the zone she was in seemed...right?

A woman could die in this kiss.

And, yes, it was nuts to be kissing this man. It was crazy to be standing in the window of his beautiful apartment overlooking all of Manhattan. It was a dream, one she surely had to wake from.

But waking was no part of her plans. He was kissing her with heat, with passion and with desire, and she had no option but to kiss him back. To do anything else would be to deny a part of her she hadn't known existed.

This was a fairy tale, she thought, in the tiny part of her mind that was available for thought. Cinders with her prince. The thought almost made her laugh, and if she wasn't being kissed maybe she would have, but the thought of not being kissed was unbearable.

So shut up, she told her consciousness. *Just kiss. Let yourself dissolve...*

And she didn't have to say it. She just did.

His strong hands were cupping her chin, holding her, lifting so his mouth could merge with hers. Her mouth was opening to welcome him.

Fire meeting fire. Strength meeting strength. Home.

For that was what this felt like. It was a wash of sensation so intense if felt as if this man, this baby, this moment was where she was meant to be for ever.

She was kissing back with an intensity that matched his. She was still cradling the baby—both of them were—and the feel of this warm, tiny bundle between them only heightened the sensation of earthquake within.

She was someone else. A woman free to love.

To be loved by Max?

Max.

Her body ached to be closer. She wanted to mould to him, to sink into him, to surrender to what she had never known she craved until this moment. If Phoebe wasn't in her arms she'd hold him tight but it didn't matter. How much closer could she be than she was right now? This was... perfect.

Scary?

No. Perfect. Right.

The night, the moment, the wash of light from the view outside, everything seemed to be dissolving. His mouth and hers formed a link fused by fire. His hands had dropped now to the small of her back, moulding her against him, but pulling her so Phoebe had the perfect cocoon.

Delicious, delectable, dangerous…

Max.

A man who was holding her with passion. Whose mouth turned her to fire. Whose eyes caressed her, loved her, told her anything was possible…

A hotel cleaner and a billionaire?

It didn't matter. It couldn't matter.

But then Phoebe stirred between them, a tiny movement, a mewed whimper, and she knew it did. Was it her consciousness that had disturbed the baby? Was Phoebe reminding her reality was right here, waiting to take hold and shake her back to where she belonged?

Which wasn't here. She'd wanted this but she had to stop. Surely she did.

Someone had to see sense and in the end it was Phoebe.

Phoebe's whimpering was telling them this moment was mad.

Phoebe whimpered and reality flooded back— and also sense.

More than anything else in the world, he wanted to pick this woman up and carry her into his bedroom. He wanted to lay her down on the welcoming covers of his king-sized bed and take this to its inevitable conclusion. For that was what it felt like. Inevitable. That his body could love her and she could love him…

But, no matter what was between them, she was here at his behest, paid to take care of his sister, paid to be alone with him. And she was alone. She had no one on this side of the world. Even though her body had moulded to his, even though she'd welcomed his kiss, had kissed him back with an intensity that matched his, a part of him was achingly aware of her vulnerability.

And…his?

If he gave himself to Sunny…

The thought was blindsiding him.

He'd had women before, of course he had, and some of those relationships had been long-standing. But every one of them had been superficial. Demanding nothing of each other but mutual enjoyment, the convenience of having a partner, decent sex. He'd been prepared to lay his cards on the table early but mostly he hadn't needed to. The women he dated were from his social milieu, out for a good time, as protective of their personal space as he was.

But Sunny… She'd want more, he thought, with insight that came from nowhere but he knew had to be the truth. She had none of the social gloss, the layers of armour, the self-sufficiency he sought in his women. She was a woman who loved, freely and without thought of self.

She could love him—but if she did she'd expect him to love her back and he didn't know how. And did he want that?

His life was organised. His childhood had taught him that independence was the only way to go. Attachment left him gutted.

And now he'd been landed with a baby. That, in itself, was huge. He'd probably end up attached; he could sense that. That scared him enough.

He looked down at the doubts in Sunny's face and he thought Phoebe was enough. To have two people dependent on him for their happiness…

He couldn't do it. He had to draw the curtain on this now.

But Sunny already had. He didn't know what she could read in his face but her face reflected… dismay? As if she'd overstepped some boundary she'd set herself and it scared her as much as it scared him.

'Wow,' she breathed, taking a step back. 'I… you pack quite a punch.'

'I'm sorry.'

And amazingly the twinkle flashed back. 'You're sorry for packing a punch?'

'I shouldn't have kissed you.'

'Why not?'

'You're my employee.' It was a lame statement and it made the twinkle disappear.

'So I am,' she said and cocked her head so she was surveying him with eyes that saw too much. 'But we're not talking of a fumble under the stairs with the kitchen maid here.'

'I wouldn't…'

'Is that how you see me? The kitchen maid?'

'Of course not.' But he didn't know where to take it.

She did, though. She gazed at him for a long minute and then gave a brisk nod. 'Okay. Don't worry. The kitchen maid isn't getting ideas. She knows you won't jump her, and in turn she won't jump you. Your boundaries are safe, and in truth they're very wise. There's a mountain between us, Max Grayland, and no one's about to knock it down because of lust.' She turned and laid Phoebe gently back into her perambulator, kissing her softly on the cheek as she tucked her in.

'Goodnight, little one,' she whispered, speaking a bit too fast. Breathlessly? 'You go and sleep by your big brother. He'll love you in the end, I know he will. He has a huge heart. He just…he just needs to figure out how big.'

And with that enigmatic statement she disappeared.

She almost ran.

Phoebe slept on. He should wheel her back to his room. Instead he stood staring at the door that led to where Sunny was…sleeping?

Could she sleep after that kiss?

Had it hit her as it'd hit him?

It didn't matter, he told himself harshly. It was just a kiss.

But it was more. What she'd just said…

How did she know him? How did she see what he was most afraid of?

He had no idea.

It must be an illusion, for how could she know when he scarcely had it figured himself?

'Go to bed,' he told himself out loud. 'Forget it. And leave her be. She's here to help for four weeks and that's it. Keep it friendly, keep it formal and keep it distant.'

And as if in protest Phoebe stirred and whimpered.

He rocked the pram for a little, then wheeled her through to his room, parking it beside his bed, then lay in his too-big bed and listened to her re-settling, the faint snuffles of a baby totally dependent on him.

Phoebe needed loving, he thought. But then he thought Phoebe needed Sunny's kind of loving. Not his.

And then he thought…

No. The idea was crazy. The idea was impossible.

He put it aside decisively and attempted to sleep.

He couldn't. The idea was still with him and it wouldn't let him rest.

It was an amazing idea. Crazy? Possibly. Probably.

'It's too soon to even think about it,' he muttered into his pillow. 'Give it time. Meanwhile, friendly, formal and distant. She needs to trust.'

And so did he, he thought, and that was a bigger ask.

Four weeks...

Maybe?

CHAPTER TEN

THE EXPEDITION TO City Hall Station took some organising. Clothes were the first thing. Both Sunny and Phoebe needed fitting out to face New York's winter. 'I can go with them,' Eliza said, but Max had his word to stick to and he did. Thus, armed with baby advice from Eliza and advice from his secretary—bemused by her boss's absence and his requests for help on women's fashion—they spent a day shopping. And doing a little exploring as well.

'I know you've seen a thousand pictures of our lady but you need to see her in person,' Max growled and the three of them took a chartered boat and sailed the harbour.

It was a practice run to see how Phoebe took to exploring and the answer was very well. Warmly ensconced in a padded carry cocoon, she allowed herself to be carried at will. She woke to feed and be cuddled and then went back to sleep again.

So Sunny was free to enjoy the day and she did enjoy it. She was dressed in the most beautiful jacket she'd ever owned, plus warm pants and sheepskin-lined boots. She was sitting in the back of a luxurious cruiser, watching the sights of New York's harbour, with Max beside her giving an intelligent and sometimes fun commentary. How could she not enjoy herself?

How could she not let herself be drawn into the illusion that there was more…?

That this man beside her was making her laugh because he cared?

That was crazy. He was being nice. He'd kissed her the night before because…well, he was a man and she was a woman and she'd practically asked for it.

He'd pulled away the moment she'd stiffened.

He was an honourable man.

She tried—hard—to stop thinking of Max the man and concentrate instead on his commentary. It containted gems that had her fascinated. Did she know that Albert Einstein's eyeballs were stored in a safe deposit box in the city? That there were tiny shrimp called copepods in Manhattan's drinking water? Or once upon a time there'd been a pneumatic mail tube system dug about four feet underground, capable of moving over ninety thousand letters a day around the whole island? 'I wish I could show you,' Max said sadly. 'But some fool seems to have dug it up.' He looked so despondent she almost giggled—okay, she did giggle—and then she thought, *Wow*, she, Sunny Raye, was being given a personalised tour of Manhattan by Max Grayland.

'Did you know all this or did you research it for the day?' she asked and he grinned.

'I asked my secretary for a list of New York's oddest. She now thinks I've lost my mind.'

And that did her head in too. She was in some sort of dream, she decided, as she gazed up at the truly magnificent Statue of Liberty. Max was right—it was far better than in the pictures.

So was Max Grayland. He had Phoebe strapped against his chest. He was smiling at her, watching her enjoy herself, wanting her to enjoy herself. She knew from his phone calls—he kept it on silent, simply glancing at the screen now and then to ensure the sky hadn't fallen—that the sky *could* almost fall at his behest and yet, not only was he sticking by his word to care for Phoebe, he was making every effort he could to ensure Sunny was having fun.

It was a dream. Australia was half a world away. She, Sunny, was having fun with a guy who, quite simply, made her toes curl.

'You're blushing,' Max said, on a note of discovery. 'What is it about our lady that makes you blush?' He glanced up at the enormous statue looming above their heads. 'As far as I can see, she's very respectably dressed.'

'I'm not blushing. I'm just…flushed.'

'Coat too hot?' he asked solicitously and, yeah, it was a lot too hot but it wasn't the coat and there wasn't a thing she could do about it.

'What…what next?' she managed.

'Empire State Building?' he queried. 'And then maybe it's time to go home.'

Home. There was another loaded word.

What was it about that statement that made her want to blush all over again?

They kept their hands off each other that night—with difficulty. *Ten out of ten*, Sunny told herself as she snuggled under her gorgeous bedclothes. She wasn't really tired but there was no way she was watching Max give Phoebe her last feed.

She had to keep her distance. Employer/employee. That was their relationship and it had to stay that way.

Except…the way he looked at her… She couldn't figure it out. It was as if he didn't understand what she was. As if he was trying to figure some puzzle that wouldn't come right. She almost asked, but whenever he caught her looking at him he'd smile and it'd make something twist inside her and she backed off in fright.

He didn't understand?

Neither did she, and it was starting to seriously scare her.

The next day they did City Hall Station.

There were tour groups that came down here—she'd read about them. Tour groups, however, were not for Max Grayland. He'd contacted a Professor of Urban Studies, Francis, a guy who'd apparently gone to university with Max, a friend who seemed to have the keys to practically all of Manhattan's underground and who professed it would be his pleasure to take them down.

'What would you like to know?' Francis asked Sunny as they trod the great underground cavern. Max stood back with Phoebe strapped to his chest and appeared to enjoy it as Sunny learned more than she'd believed possible about New York's network of rail tunnels. Past, present, future. Francis knew the entire history, everything she could possibly want to know. She drank it in, and for a while she even forgot Max was watching.

'You need someone with architecture knowledge as well,' Francis told her. He turned back to Max. 'Max, you know Tom Clifford? Anything you want to know about historical tunnelling, he's your man, and I believe he'll be in town this weekend. How about you and Sunny come to dinner? Tom and Sunny can go hammer and tongs and the rest of us can learn and enjoy.'

'I don't…we don't go out,' Sunny said, too fast. Oh, for heaven's sake, as if she was part of Max Grayland's social life… 'Phoebe…'

'Hmm, yeah.' Francis smiled benignly at the sleeping bundle on Max's chest. 'My wife and I have three rug rats. They do cramp your style. But surely you have a nanny.'

'I'm the nanny,' Sunny managed.

'She's not.' Max had hardly spoken but he intervened now, putting a hand on Sunny's shoulder. And why the touch should go through her…

She was wearing three layers of padding to protect her from the creeping cold associated with being so far underground. There was no way she should feel it.

She felt it as if his fingers were on her naked skin.

She shuddered, and Max felt it.

'Time to go up,' he decreed. 'No, Sunny's not a nanny; she's a friend helping out until I find one. But dinner sounds a great idea. At my place. Francis, you and your wife? Tom and his partner? Anyone else who'd enjoy the conversation?'

'Mary Rutherford's into the history of the rail network. She's great company. I could persuade her.'

'Max…' Sunny said, feeling desperate. 'I can't…'

'Hey, there's nothing to this,' Max reassured her. 'This is Manhattan. There's a whole world of caterers out there. I'll have my secretary organise it. All you need to do, Sunny, is sit back and enjoy it.'

'That's not what I'm here for.'

'Yes, it is,' he told her and he smiled, and such a smile… It was all she could do not to gasp. But the smile had been fleeting and he'd turned back to Francis. 'So… Saturday? Anyone else you can think of who Sunny might enjoy grilling? I might need to do some pre-dinner research to keep up.'

And it was done.

Saturday night. Sunny had thrown every objection she could think of at him and he'd overruled them all.

The final one had been dress and that was the biggest hurdle. He and Phoebe had escorted her to the salon his secretary had told him of and she'd looked at the prices and almost had kittens.

'No way,' she'd declared, walking straight out. 'With that sort of money I could buy a new wheelchair for Pa. Not a dress for a night.'

'I'll pay for a wheelchair anyway,' he growled and she looked at him as if he'd lost his mind.

'You're my boss, not my sugar daddy. But, seeing you've organised this dinner...' He'd given her a credit card as promised and now she took it from her purse and looked at it doubtfully. 'You're sure I can use this?'

'Absolutely. It's part of the deal.'

'You've already bought me cold weather gear. But now...if I can take a couple of hours off...'

'Of course.'

'I promise I won't abuse it.'

'I'd enjoy watching you abuse it.'

'The coat was bad enough,' she retorted. 'Having you watch while I try on slinky gowns...'

'I'd definitely enjoy it.'

She'd grinned, but it was a grin that put him in his place. It said sexy banter was just that, banter, and he needed to shut up.

So he shut up and hoped she'd choose something that wouldn't make her feel like a poor relation when she met for dinner with people he knew had style and impeccable taste and confidence.

But when she emerged from her room on Saturday night she took his breath away.

She was wearing a dress of silver-grey lace, a frock that would have been equally at home in a nineteen-twenties drawing room as it was here. It was a simple tube, scoop-necked, reaching to just above her knees. The tube consisted entirely of circles of fringing, soft, silky and delicate, and it shimmered as she moved, so even though the dress itself seemed shapeless, somehow it accentuated every one of her delicious curves.

She was wearing silver court shoes with kitten heels. A single rope of some kind of white shell that shimmered like pearls. Tiny matched earrings.

Her hair had been let loose. It was tucked behind her ears but cascaded to her shoulders in a mass of shiny curls.

Her make-up was simple—a touch of lipstick, a brush of blush to accentuate her beautiful cheekbones.

She looked so lovely she took his breath away.

'How…how is it?' she asked a little self-consciously and he didn't answer for a moment. He couldn't.

But she looked worried. 'I found it in a vintage shop in Soho and it was a bit battered,' she told him. 'I had to sew a lot of the lace back on but I love it. It's not too much for tonight? They won't think I'm doing a fancy dress?'

'They will *not* think you're doing a fancy dress,' he breathed and then the doorbell pealed and it was the caterers and waiting staff he'd hired for the occasion, and it was just as well because if they hadn't arrived then, who knew what would have happened?

All Max knew was that he felt as if he'd just been punched. Hard. Or was that the wrong word? Wrong metaphor—punched?

Knocked sideways.

He wanted to lock the door, lock the world out and spend the night alone with this woman. He wanted to touch her bare shoulders, draw her to him, feel the soft silk mould to his body.

And the idea that had been an embryo just days ago was growing. It was starting to become… something that seemed a consummation devoutly to be wished?

If he could pull it off…

But he needed to keep his hands off her now. He needed not to scare her, to keep things businesslike, to let her see how they could make things work.

But meanwhile the caterers were heading for the kitchen and Sunny was looking doubtful, as if she really imagined her appearance might be inappropriate. Which was so far from the truth...

'You look beautiful,' he told her and he thought of the minuscule amount he'd seen when he'd checked his credit card details after her shopping expedition. He'd come close to demanding to see what she'd bought so he could march her out to buy something more suitable—but no money in the world could make her look more beautiful than she did right now. 'You're perfect,' he added and she blushed and the temptation to kiss her was so great...

'Thank you,' she said simply. 'I'll check on Phoebe before the guests arrive.'

'I can do that.'

'That's what I'm here for,' she said, almost sternly. 'You're being incredibly generous but I'm not about to forget my role.' The doorbell pealed again and she nodded, affirming the truth for herself. 'Go and greet your guests, Max,' she told him. 'I'll meet you in the dining room, as long as Phoebe doesn't need me.'

Phoebe was sound asleep. The baby monitor was routed to the dining room. There was nothing for Sunny to do but return.

She didn't for a while, though. She stood and gazed down at the sleeping baby. She thought of Max greeting guests, in his jet-black Italian suit with crisp white shirt, his silk tie, a billionaire at the top of his game. And she thought of the way he'd looked at her.

I need to be so careful. She almost whispered it aloud but the intercom was on and she wasn't so far gone to forget where she was.

Or who she was.

I'm here to do a job, she told herself as she listened to the sound of arriving guests, of Max meeting them with the ease of long-standing friendship or, in the case of those he hadn't met, with the assurance of his place in the world.

I'm a hotel cleaner, she told herself. *Remember it. Max has invited these people to meet you. Which is very good of him. If I ever get to study architecture they might... I might...*

But the impossibility of *might* was enough to bring her to her senses. She knew why she was here and she knew what she was going home to.

It's just a dinner, she told herself. *With a boss who's being charming to an employee. So the boss kissed the chambermaid? That's the way things have been since time immemorial. Get over it, Sunny. Move on.*

The voices from the dining room seemed relaxed. There was laughter, banter, ease of social standing.

*So stay in the background like a good little em-
ployee*, she told herself. *Know your place. Okay,
Sunny Raye, big breath. You can do this.*

But heaven only knew the courage it took to
walk through that door.

For the first part of the dinner Sunny seemed deliberately retiring. The talk was general as his
guests got to know each other, friendly and un-
threatening. Sunny was asked about her home in
Australia, her thoughts on New York, but mostly
she was left alone. She seemed to want it that way.

After the main course Phoebe woke and Sunny
excused herself. Through the intercom they heard
Sunny's soft crooning as Phoebe fed and then settled.

'She's some lady.' His friend, Francis, had listened to her in the tunnel and had been impressed.
Now he was eyeing Max with speculation. Max
tried for a non-committal shrug but Francis had
known him for a long time. Maybe he saw…what
he was thinking?

And when Sunny returned it was Francis who
deliberately brought Sunny into the conversation.
He led the discussion to the tunnels underpinning
Manhattan, and from there to the history of tunnelling, to the architecture involved, to the engineering that formed the foundations for almost
every city in the world.

Who'd have thought tunnels could be so fascinating? Max thought. Maybe they weren't, but he was fascinated with Sunny's response.

They were talking of the Lincoln Tunnel, built in the nineteen-thirties to carry traffic under the Hudson. 'There may be problems in the future,' Francis was saying and Sunny nodded. Her decision to stay in the background faltered in the face of Francis's determination to have her join in.

'Battery Park City,' she murmured and Francis eyed her cautiously.

'You know the problems?'

'I guess…' She seemed almost embarrassed.

'I don't know of any problems,' Max said and she cast him a look that was almost resentful. She'd asked questions as they'd talked and they'd been intelligent but she'd been backward in contributing. He thought that it had been like that at Christmas, probably for most of her life. Sunny's siblings were deemed the 'intelligent' ones, the ones with the education. Sunny stayed in the background and listened.

But she was caught now, by Francis's interest and by Max's direct probe. He watched her hesitate, almost as if she was afraid to reveal what she knew. But the interest around her was friendly. She'd had a couple of glasses of wine.

He almost saw her give a mental shrug.

'The Hudson River's main current has always been close to the edge of Lower Manhattan,' she told him. 'As far as I understand, building Battery Park City has rerouted it. The current's now closer to the river centre and it's washing away much of the soil on the walls and ceiling of the tunnel. It means they're a lot more susceptible to shifting and cracking. It's a huge problem the world over—a demonstration of why city planners need to take a broader view. When the initial rail tunnels were built there was an overview of every surface and underground construction. Now…it's like a rabbit warren as each developer fights for space.' She eyed him speculatively, almost challengingly. 'The Grayland Corporation has fingers in Battery Park projects, I believe. And you're not aware of it?'

She arched an eyebrow, gently quizzing, and beside her Francis gave a snort of laughter. 'Well, well. A lady with an overview of the entire Grayland Corporation—in your own home. You're in trouble, Max.'

This was his father's legacy. He'd already taken steps to counter such problems in the future, so now he could grin and hold up his hands in surrender. He could defend his company's structural sensitivities and move on.

The moment passed but the conversation had changed. Sunny was now a respected participant.

She was no longer the nanny. Not even close. As they talked of the difficulties of maintaining past tunnels and building new ones, as they discussed soil density and rock formation and river flow, as they talked of population growth and the need to accommodate more, she held her own and pushed further.

She hadn't learned all this in the last few days, he thought, stunned. How much had she stored in that head of hers while she'd scrubbed floors?

He found himself resenting it when others spoke. All he wanted was to listen, sit back and watch. She was smart, funny, quick. She was warm, loyal, loving.

She was perfect.

She was a woman he'd never thought he'd meet. *A woman he'd be proud to call his...wife?*

He sat as the conversation washed around him and let the concept drift.

Three weeks ago he'd been single, schooled in independence by a cold, isolated upbringing. That had been okay. Independence had its own rewards.

But Phoebe's arrival had changed that. He'd had a choice: adopt the child and rear her with love, or walk away. He hadn't been able to walk, and his precious independence was shattered.

But then came Sunny. This woman was a lifesaver. She'd rescued him from a situation that did his head in. She'd shown him how to love, what warmth was, what commitment was, and he wanted it. He wanted it for Phoebe and now...

as he watched her he thought he wanted it for himself.

And the thought was there, a selfish niggle but one that stayed reassuringly in place. With Sunny here as his wife, as Phoebe's…mom…he could go back to the life he knew. His commitment to his financial empire could stay unchanged. He'd not have the emotional burden of thinking Phoebe was home with a paid nanny. He wouldn't have to check and check again, or go through the emotional turmoil he remembered as a child when a beloved nanny left.

And when he did come home…this place would be different. Sunny would be here as she was now, smart, feisty, welcoming. They could still hire a nanny, but part-time. Sunny could study her beloved architecture but that'd be in college hours. When he got home she'd be here.

Family. Ready-built.

And it'd be great for her. The change to her life would be amazing. No more scrubbing… He could help her family back home…

The concept got better and better, and Francis glanced across the table at him and raised his brows.

'You're looking smug.'

'Smug?' *Uh-oh.* He schooled his expression with haste. There were things he needed to put in place before he could afford to look smug. Like asking her.

But how could she say no? He knew she was as attracted to him as he was to her. He could feel it. They'd lived together for weeks now, first at her grandparents' house and then here. He could feel the frisson of sexual tug that happened whenever they came close.

'I like it when a plan comes together,' he admitted to Francis. 'Like this dinner. You guys seem to be hitting it off.'

'I'm taking Sunny for a tour of a couple of our old rail tunnels the general public don't know about,' Francis told him. 'We'll organise it as soon as she has a day off.'

'A day off?'

'Isn't Sunny working as your nanny?'

'Sunny's not a nanny,' he growled, almost roughly. 'Sunny's my…godsend. Sunny's my friend.'

She didn't feel like a friend.

The dinner over, guests and caterers departed, Max did a fast check on his emails and went to find Sunny. She was watching a sleeping Phoebe.

She'd kicked off her shoes. She was still wearing her beautiful dress. Her curls were soft and shining. He stood at the door and watched her in the dim light, bent almost protectively over the cot.

They'd moved the cot into his room now. The

room was massive. A vast bed. A cot with a sleeping baby. Moonlight playing in the window and a beautiful woman standing guard.

He walked slowly forward and placed his hands on her waist. He felt her stiffen but only for a moment. He felt the instant she decided to relax, the moment her body leaned back into his, the instant her loveliness curved against his chest.

'It was a great night,' he said softly and he couldn't help himself; he buried his face into her curls and kissed her.

'It was.' But was she trembling?

He turned her to face him. She looked troubled. Doubtful. Scared?

'Sunny, I won't...if you don't want this...'

'That's just the problem,' she whispered. 'I know it's dumb. I know it's unwise, but oh, Max, I do want this.'

'Then as one consenting adult to another...' He cupped her chin and kissed her lips, a kiss so tender it almost blew him away. He didn't know he could kiss like this. He didn't know he could care. 'Sunny, as one consenting adult to another, would you do me the very great honour of coming to my bed?'

She drew back a little, watching him in the moonlight, her face still troubled.

'Because?'

'Because I want you,' he said honestly because there was no room for anything but honesty between them right now. 'But Sunny, it's more. I think… I think I'm starting to love you.'

'Well, how about that?' Her voice was a breathless whisper. 'How about that for a miracle, Max Grayland? Because…because I think I'm starting to love you, too.'

CHAPTER ELEVEN

WHAT FOLLOWED WAS two weeks of time out of frame. Two weeks of fantasy.

For two weeks they were a make-believe family. Max seemed to drop almost everything and devote himself to her and to Phoebe.

With Phoebe strapped securely against Max's chest, they explored New York in winter.

Every morning when she woke Sunny was presented with a list of things he thought might be fun. Museums. Art galleries. A flea market. A New Year firecracker ceremony. A winter jazz festival. A snow carnival with ice carving. They were hers to choose, but Max put himself behind every one of them with enthusiasm and enjoyment.

They'd even ended up at a knitting festival where he'd tried his hand, then bought wool and declared his intention of knitting Phoebe a scarf. She'd watched him that night, laboriously casting on and dropping stitches while they waited up for Phoebe's last feed. In helpless laughter, with the wool a tangled knot, they'd made a mutual decision that knitting wasn't their forte.

She'd watched him carefully untangle the knot. She'd thought of the business empire this man controlled and her sense of fantasy had deepened.

But how could she care that it was fantasy? She was so in love.

For every night he took her to his bed and she fell deeper and deeper…

Max Grayland. A fantasy?

Her love.

How could she leave? She knew she must, but she wouldn't—she couldn't think of it yet.

A week before she was due to leave she woke in his arms and her sense of peace and contentment was all-enveloping. Fantasy seemed real and she let herself believe. How could she not? The morning light started to filter though the half-closed curtains. She was warm, she was sated—she was sleeping in the arms of the man she loved.

She'd never thought this could happen to her and, miraculously, it seemed to be returned. The way Max held her…the way he looked at her, laughed with her, loved her…

Her body seemed his and vice versa. From the moment he'd lifted her joyously and carried her to his bed it seemed as if this was her place. This was where she'd been meant to be all her life.

How could this be fantasy?

And yet it was. She knew that. Her life was half a world away, and yet who was thinking forward? Not her. She couldn't bear to. Only here and now mattered.

Phoebe lay sleeping in her crib on the far side of the room, a contented cherub who had no idea she'd been abandoned. Who acted as if she'd been loved all her life.

So what of the future?

Forget the future, Sunny told herself. For now she was milking this moment for everything it was worth, taking Max's love and savouring it because...because...

There was no *because*. There was no need to worry about the future. It was all *now*.

Her face was resting on Max's chest. It should be an uncomfortable sleeping position but Max's arms held her, supported her, cradled her body against him as if she were the most precious thing...

What it was to be precious in this man's eyes...

'Awake already?' he whispered, his voice teasing, and she knew his eyes would already be glinting with laughter. In these last weeks there'd been so much...joy.

Joy to last a lifetime.

Do not think forward.

'I'm dozing,' she whispered back. 'Don't move. I think I'm in heaven.'

'Really?'

'Okay, I know I'm in heaven.'

'Me too,' he whispered but he did move and it was entirely appropriate that he did because heaven just got better.

Love... She let it take her where it would. Her surrender—and his—was complete.

When finally they surfaced the sun was streaming in. It was a stunningly perfect winter's day. Phoebe was still sleeping but soon she'd stir. Their day would begin.

Seven days to go…

The last weeks had been…heaven. Sure, they'd had a tiny baby to care for but somehow she'd fitted right into their plans—right into their hearts?

'I'd like to walk all the way around Central Park today,' she ventured. There'd been so many things she'd seen, but the weather hadn't permitted a full circuit.

'Can we do that tomorrow? The forecast is for this weather to hold.' He was holding her close, hugging her as if she belonged. Skin against skin… It was the most erotic sensation in the world. 'Sunny…my secretary's lined up nanny interviews this afternoon. I'd like you to sit in.'

'Of course.' That was what she was here for after all, but the thought was an intrusion, an acknowledgment that what was happening now was a dream. Time out of frame. A nanny would take over. Max would return to his high-pressure world.

She'd go…home.

'But first…' He kissed her gently on the lips, a feather touch, a touch of such intimacy she could weep. 'If it's okay… I've organised time out, something just for us. Eliza's coming in to look after Phoebe. The nanny appointments are scheduled from three and after, so we'll have time together.'

'You've planned this.'

'I have.' Once more he kissed her. 'Sunny, I need this day to be even more special than it is already.'

And then he gathered her even closer, the kiss became deeper, the need became more urgent... and there was no room for questions. There was room only for each other.

He wouldn't tell her where they were going. 'Wear what you wore underground,' he said and he dressed that way as well, in a cool leather jacket, casual pants, a cashmere scarf that made him look...

Okay, she shouldn't think of how he looked.

His car—with chauffeur—dropped them at the Rockefeller Center.

'How are you on ice?' he asked as he led her through the complex and she stopped so fast the couple walking behind them almost bumped into them.

'Ice?'

'I thought we might skate.'

'You're kidding.'

'This is the coolest ice rink in the world.'

'And I don't skate. I've never seen ice bigger than little cubes you put in drinks.'

'You don't rollerblade? Ski?'

She didn't move, all the memories of her rubbish childhood flooding back. Watching other kids skateboard and rollerblade. Listening to kids telling tales of how their parents had taken them to the admittedly sparse Australian ski fields. Saving so she could buy roller skates for her siblings.

Not for her.

'No,' she said shortly. And then she thought that was no reason to spoil what for him seemed a very exciting plan. 'But it'll be fun to watch you.'

'I have no intention of letting you watch,' he told her and there was that smile again. 'I pretty much guessed you'd have no experience. I was just checking. Will you trust me? This'll be fun.'

Really? Fun for who?

But Max wasn't listening to her protests. He led her on until the vast ice rink stretched before them. It wasn't crowded—apparently Tuesday morning wasn't the time for most people to skate—but there were enough skaters flying around the rink, spinning, doing figures of eight, totally at ease with their environment, for her doubts to consolidate into one great wall of objection.

'I can't.'

'But I can,' he said gently and then he asked again. 'Trust me?'

Oh, for heaven's sake... She'd break a leg. She'd have her fingers sliced off. She'd be carried home in a box...

'I won't let that happen,' he said and she almost glared. How dare this man see what she was thinking? Was she so transparent?

'Trust me,' he said for the third time, and she gazed into his face. She thought of the warmth, the heat, the strength of this body she was starting to know and love so much and there was only one answer.

But first a quibble. 'My pet goldfish...' she murmured.

'What?'

'I need a pen and paper to write an advanced directive. If I die Daisy will want her, because she's the responsible one, but she won't talk to her and Flippy likes to chat. Flippy goes to Sam.'

'You're planning on writing a will—right here and now?'

'I want it legal,' she told him. 'A paper napkin will do and a couple of random skaters for witnesses.'

'Okay,' he said faintly. 'But then you'll skate?'

'You swear I'll come out in one piece?'

'I swear.'

'I hold you to your promise but you never know. Flippy gets catered for first.'

So minutes later...skates on, standing—shakily—at the edge of the gorgeous rink, looking at skilled skaters using every inch of the ice, looking at the magnificent golden statue at the end of the rink, seeing the myriad sightseers watching the skaters...

She was ready?

She was so unready it was ridiculous.

'Max…'

'Trust me,' he said for the fourth time and his arm came around her waist, strong and sure. 'Relax and let me guide you. Come on, Sunny, let's fly.' And that's exactly what happened. Somehow, some way, she was out on the ice, flying over its surface, held tightly against Max… She was…skating.

She was really skating!

Or… not. If he was a matador, she was the cape, but in his skilled hands she moved as if she was born on the rink.

This man was seriously good. He skated as if it was a part of him—and she was another part. Or maybe not a part. Maybe she'd melted into him, been absorbed, just… Sunny and Max.

For the first few seconds she fought to relax, she had to school herself to trust him, but as she felt his skill, as she felt his strength and certainty, she found herself relaxing. More. Enjoying.

Loving?

For that was what this was. It was subjugation of her body to his but in a way that could only bring joy. She could think of nothing but this moment. There was no future, no past, simply this man spinning her around, moving her with a deftness that made her feel…

Like Torvill and Dean? The image of the world-famous Olympians sprang to mind and she almost choked on laughter. If she simply let Max do what he willed…

'What's funny?' he asked into her hair as they spun seamlessly together and she smiled back. Her body was moulded to his. If he let her go she'd be a puddle on the ice in seconds, but he wouldn't let her go. She knew it. She knew this man.

'I'm thinking Olympics R Us,' she managed and he chuckled and held her tighter.

'It's the together,' he told her. 'Together we can do anything we like. The world is ours, Sunny Raye. Let's just enjoy it.'

And she did.

Could he do this? Take this one last step?

As he held her and skated, he felt his world almost dissolve in love and laughter and desire. But it didn't quite dissolve. There remained a part of him that was almost separate, watching from above, seeing what he was doing and testing it for sense.

The sensible part of him, the part that had formed from childhood, turning finally and harshly into a dark, aloof entity the day they'd wrenched a pup from him and told him to grow up, that part said it was risky.

Could he do this? Could he love this woman and keep himself safe?

There were so many positives. Sunny would

gain so much. Phoebe would grow up without that dark fear he had. And he...

He'd have Sunny beside him, curled against him in the dark, trusting, loving...

He could love her. He could keep her safe. They could be a family.

The two sides of him had warred since he'd met her, but now, holding her close as they spun, as she laughed and held him, as he felt her warmth, her trust...

He could love her. He would. The two sides of him could find some way of moving forward.

Some things were worth the risk.

She was so exhausted she could hardly speak. She was so in love...

When even Max was breathless, he led her from the rink, helped her remove her skates and took her to a tiny café high up, overlooking the rink, seemingly overlooking the whole of Manhattan.

They ate pancakes, piled high with creamed butter and maple syrup, with vast bowls of strawberries on the side. They drank coffee like Sunny had never tasted before. Nothing had ever tasted like this before. The world seemed to have changed. It was no longer her world. It was a fantasy.

And then, as the waiter cleared their dishes, as they were left in their private space, Max leaned over and took her hand.

And then, just as she thought the fantasy couldn't get any better, he opened his other hand.

A box.

Crimson velvet.

Tiny.

He flicked it open and he smiled into her eyes with such tenderness she forgot to breathe. How could she breathe? Did she need to when this was a fairy tale?

But he was speaking. Somehow she had to pretend it was real.

Somehow she had to catch her breath.

'Sunny Raye,' he said, softly but surely. 'I can't think of a better time or a better place. I've fallen deeply in love with you, so deeply that I never want to let you go. So there's only one question to ask. Will you do me the very great honour of becoming my wife?'

My wife...

A ring...

She felt as if she'd been shifted into a parallel universe.

He was handing her a ring.

How could she get her voice to work?

What was she supposed to say? Was she supposed to pretend this fairy tale was real?

Yes! Every single fibre of her being screamed it. She wanted the fairy tale. She gazed down at the perfect diamond set in white gold, and the compulsion to slip it on her finger was so great it was like a physical force.

To marry this man she loved… To love Max Grayland for ever…

But in the end it was the skating that made her hesitate. It was the skating that made her look up into Max's eyes, to see the love, but also something else.

And some survival instinct played back his words. *I never want to let you go.*

The skating… He'd held her close. She'd been safe and she'd had fun but he'd been totally in control.

This was his world.

I never want to let you go.

So instead of looking mistily into his eyes and whispering what her heart most wanted—*Yes!*—she found another part of her answering. A part she didn't want to acknowledge, but there seemed no choice.

'How…how would that work?' She could barely get the words out. 'Max…how could marriage to me possibly work?'

'Brilliantly.' He was still holding her hand. The ring still lay on its bed of velvet, a siren song. It would be so easy to slip it on.

'But…how?'

'I have it planned. That's why I needed to talk to you before we interview the nannies this afternoon. I thought I'd need a full-time nanny but…'

'But you'll marry me instead?'

'That's not the way I'd ever intend it,' he said, suddenly harsh, in a voice that said he spoke absolute truth. 'I don't need to marry you to provide a nanny for Phoebe. I hope you know me better than that.'

'Then…'

'But we'll still need one.' His hold on her hand tightened.

She looked into his face and she thought, *He has this all figured.* She'd come in on this late. He had his plans in place.

'You want to study architecture,' he told her. 'That can be arranged.'

'I don't have schooling…'

'You'd pass every entrance test they could ever devise and I can pull strings. I can get you in. You can do it part-time if you like—that'd give you time to catch up on gaps you might have—or full-time if you want. That's why we need to think about what we need the nanny for. I need to go back to work and give it my total commitment. I'll cut back a bit—of course—but I can't be depended on to be here for Phoebe. But you'd be here for her. The nanny would do the hard yards but she'd have you to love. And when I come home… we'll be a family.'

'When you come home…'

'I'll do the best I can,' he told her. 'But my job's huge. But Sunny, think. Us. Family. No more cleaning. No more scrubbing your hands raw and worrying about money. I can take care of your grandparents…'

'Now that's something I don't understand.' And suddenly something inside her was growing angry. She hardly understood but the world was starting to look…a little bit red? 'How can you do that? Chloe and Tom are due to go back to university at the end of summer. They lead their own lives. Are you intending to keep paying them to stay on with Gran and Pa?'

'I can afford a carer—a good one. You can fly home and do the interviewing if you like. In fact you'd probably like to marry from there. I can take a little more time off if you need my help. We can take Phoebe with us, take the time to set things up to make them safe.'

'By employing strangers.' Her voice sounded hollow.

The ring was still on the table. The joy she'd felt on seeing it had disappeared completely. It seemed to be mocking her.

Why? Why couldn't she just say yes? She could fall into his arms. She could live in his beautiful apartment for ever. She could love a little girl she… Well, to be honest, she already did love.

She could love a man she already did love.

'Sunny…' The hold on her hand was compelling. 'You've put yourself last almost from the

time of your birth. You've done everything for
your family that you possibly could. It's time to
let me help.'

'By employing strangers.'

'By letting me make them safe. By giving you
the chance to stop being a martyr.'

'Is that what you think I am—a martyr?'

'Yes,' he said gently. 'You've done it for love
but you're a martyr nevertheless. I love you for
it but I won't let you continue. It's Sunny's time.'

'I don't think…' She was struggling to get her
mind to work. 'Max, I don't think doing anything
for love can possibly be martyrdom. It's just what
you do.'

'And you have done it. But it's done. Dusted.
It's time for you to stop being needed.'

'So if I lived with you… I wouldn't be needed.'

'You'd be loved—of course you'd be loved. But
I wouldn't let Phoebe's needs stand in the way of
your ambitions. We'll employ the right nanny so
you can be as involved as you want.'

'But I wasn't talking about Phoebe.' Still her
voice sounded hollow. Dull. She knew it but there
wasn't a thing she could do about it. 'I was talking
about you. Would you need me, Max?'

'I want you.'

'That's not the same.'

'Haven't you had enough of being needed?'

'Yes. No!' She was so confused. The tenderness, the romance of the moment was gone.

'Sunny, not everyone needs like your family does.'

'You don't need anyone?'

'I've worked on that. Needing causes pain and I won't go there. But Sunny, loving you...it'd bring joy...'

'In the time we had available. The time between your business commitments. These weeks... they've been a time out for you, but you want to go back.'

'I have to go back.'

'To your business.'

'It's what I am.'

'And there's the difference.' She was struggling to speak, struggling to get the words out. 'My work isn't what I am.'

'Because you're a cleaner.'

'That's insulting. As if what I do isn't important...'

'How can it be?'

'Because it's just work? And yours is different?' She rose, pushing her chair back so fast it almost fell. The knot of anger inside her couldn't be contained. But was it anger?

It was desolation. It was a sinking sense of certainty. It was the knowledge that the ring lying on the table could never be hers.

She took a deep breath and struggled to stay calm. To be still. To say it like it was.

'What's important is family,' she told him. 'I understand...you've never had that so you don't know. You've made yourself believe that independence is the most important thing, but believe me...' She closed her eyes. 'The day after Mum died... When the social workers came and took the kids to foster homes... They told me they'd be safe and cared for and that was the most important thing, but I was fourteen years old and I knew it wasn't. Even at fourteen I knew that love was bigger, and I knew I'd give up everything to get it right. Tell me, Max, what will you do if—when—Phoebe needs you? Will you drop anything and go to her? Or will you send a nanny?'

'If she really needs...'

'Define *needs*,' she said harshly. 'Does she have to fall under a bus for that need to kick in? What if she just needs a cuddle? Or someone to read to her every night?'

'If it's minor...' He was hopelessly out of his depth and she knew it. He didn't understand, and it was useless trying to change it.

The situation was impossible. The whole thing was impossible.

She reached down and flipped the top of the crimson box closed. It closed with a snap that seemed to resound through the restaurant.

Dream over.

'It can't work,' she said dully. 'This time...for me it's been magic. A dream. But that's all it can be, a dream. I wish for Phoebe's sake—and, okay, for ours—that I could say yes but I'd be giving up too much. Gran and Pa need me. Daisy and Sam and Chloe and Tom are part of what I am. They're my family. Yes, they can put too many demands on me, and yes, sometimes I resent it, but love goes both ways. I need them as much as they need me. Living with you… Loving a man who gives and gives and never acknowledges that need is a part of loving too…' She shook her head. 'Okay, I'm not making sense. I can see that you don't understand and I can't help. But please…accept it's over. Let's go interview these nannies because we need one soon. I'm going home, Max. I'm going back to where I belong.'

There was no way to dissuade her.

They worked their way through the list of nannies. Sunny was a great interviewer. She asked questions he would never have thought of.

How are you at cuddles? What's your favourite kids' storybook? What would you do if the kindergarten teacher phoned and said Phoebe's just bitten someone? How do you feel about puppies? What do you feel is the most important part of your job?

The one who stood out was Karen, a single mum with a toddler of her own, Harry.

'How do you feel about living in if you get the job?' Sunny asked and Max pretty much froze. To have two kids…

But Karen was warm and caring, and as she left Sunny turned to him and said, 'She's perfect.'

And he knew she was. He'd been around Sunny long enough now to know what perfect was.

Only Sunny was more perfect.

'And she can start now,' Sunny said in satisfaction. 'Which means I can go home.'

'I don't want you to go home.'

'That's where I'm needed,' she told him and before he could say anything more she'd backed away and headed to the sanctuary of her own room.

A room she hadn't used for two weeks because she'd slept with him.

Her rejection had him stunned. What was between them was so right. She was everything he'd ever wanted in a woman. Their bodies meshed. Her intelligence blew him away. Her warmth and humour reached parts of him he hadn't known existed.

He could offer her so much and yet her rejection of his offer had been instantaneous.

She'd said no and she meant it. She was going home and he had no way of stopping her.

Except by changing.

But how could she expect him to change when he didn't have a clue what she was on about?

He was gutted but he was also…angry? To throw away what he was offering…

Don't think about it, he told himself. *It's her*

choice. Head into the study, draw up a contract for the new nanny and then get on with your life.

Move on alone, as you always have. You should know by now that it's the only way.

And, as if on cue, while Sunny lay sleepless, staring at the ceiling, her cell phone rang.

Chloe.

'Sunny, Pa's had another stroke. Not…not fatal, we think. We hope. We're not even sure how bad it is but…we thought you'd want to know.'

'Oh, Chloe…' Sunny heard sobs suppressed behind her sister's voice. They matched the sobs she'd been trying to suppress herself.

'I'll come home,' she said.

'I don't think… I wish I could say…'

'Don't say anything at all,' Sunny told her. 'I'm coming.'

She disconnected. Then she headed for the bathroom and washed her face.

The light showed under Max's door. She knocked and asked for his help.

At eight the next morning the jet took off, heading for Australia.

The dream was over. She was on her way home.

CHAPTER TWELVE

IT WAS A huge day in the life of Phoebe Raye Grayland.

And of Max.

The adoption had taken almost a year to organise but this afternoon Max had stood in front of a judge with Phoebe in his arms. He'd promised to provide her with a loving home, for ever and ever.

He'd expected it to be a formality, a simple signing of documents. Instead, as the attorney had asked him to confirm before the judge his intention to love her and care for her, he'd felt something shift inside him. Something huge.

And then the judge had taken Phoebe from him and dandled her, and told Max how lucky he was. He'd let Phoebe have the gavel and Phoebe had banged it with gusto.

The documents were signed and sealed. Phoebe was his.

Family.

The feeling was almost overwhelming.

He should send the picture of Phoebe and the gavel to Sunny.

Would she like it that he'd added her name to Phoebe's?

He'd taken the full day off to mark the occasion. Karen and her Harry were out Christmas shopping.

Max was pushing a dozy Phoebe in her stroller, feeling…discombobulated. As if he wasn't sure how to feel.

Manhattan looked like one blazing Christmas tree, albeit an oddly shaped one. Cold had descended in earnest. There were flurries of snow in the air. Phoebe was currently wearing the cutest little Christmas hat, half beanie, half muffler.

Eliza had bought it for her. Karen had decreed it was the cutest thing and Phoebe loved its furriness. A week ago he'd arrived home to find both women clucking over his half-sister, and Phoebe grinning toothily at both of them. She'd pretty much worn it night and day since.

He'd done okay by her. She was loved.

So now she was his. *His.*

For some reason he couldn't go home. He needed this time, pushing his little sister through the throng of Christmas shoppers. To look at the shops. To lose himself…

To think of Christmas.

To think of what was happening back in Australia?

Except he shouldn't be wondering. He knew. Once a week he had an email from Sunny, outlining how things were. Her grandfather had pulled up after the stroke, weakened but still essentially okay. The new gardener he'd insisted on paying for was doing magnificently and the house repairs were very much appreciated. How was Phoebe doing?

They were grateful emails. She was embarrassed that he was doing so much, though there was so much he'd like to do that she wouldn't permit. He was permitted to help Gran and Pa, but not her. Nothing personal.

Her emails were thus filled with gratitude, plus concern and care for a child she'd learned to love.

They contained nothing to admit she might love him.

He wrote back in the same style. They'd become…friends?

At his insistence she told him the basics. She was back at the hotel, working, but she'd been promoted. She was now a team leader, so scrubbing floors was no longer part of her usual duties. She only scrubbed occasionally, in a crisis.

She was doing another subject at night school.

She was still bicycling to work, caring for her grandparents, worrying about her siblings.

Preparing for Christmas.

He'd ordered a hamper to be sent. It was filled with the most indulgent delicacies money could buy. He'd topped it with another truly extravagant box of cherry liqueur chocolates and he'd sent it in plenty of time to reach them.

Except as soon as he'd sent it he'd had doubts. Was part of Gran's pleasure in receiving the sweets the fact that Sunny gave them to her? Had Sunny already bought a cheaper version?

He was second-guessing himself and that was pretty much how he was these days. In unfamiliar territory.

In his business world he was crisp, incisive, authoritarian. His father's legacy of dubious business dealings was over. The Grayland financial empire was going from strength to strength. In the financial world, Max Grayland was a man in charge.

But he came home at night and Phoebe reached her little arms up to be cuddled and doubts crept in. He held her close, he snuggled her warm little person, he admired the new skills she'd learned that day and he wanted…someone to share.

Karen and Eliza were great but…

But yesterday Phoebe had pushed herself to a wobbly standing position. Today he'd formally adopted her. Both were huge milestones in the life of Phoebe.

And he'd wanted…he'd ached for Sunny to be there. To share it with him.

He'd taken today off but last night he'd reached home at eight, and he'd had ten minutes admiring Phoebe's new standing skill before she'd slept.

Sunny would have expected—needed—him to be home before that because Sunny needed a family. She hadn't emailed him yet this week and he guessed it was because she was caught up with Christmas preparations. He thought of the vast

Christmas table at her grandparents' house, of the preparation, of the work she'd be doing to make this Christmas wonderful.

And he had to fight back a longing so powerful it made him stop dead in the street.

A Christmas tree bumped into him and apologies were everywhere. The tree—Mum and Dad under it, three kids trailing behind—went on its way and he watched its going.

Christmas trees were being half towed, half carried along the snow-covered streets, lugged by laughing friends, mums and dads, grandpas, tribes of kids. Young women breezed past him in bright, happy groups, laden with Christmas shopping. An elderly lady slipped on the icy pavement and her husband fell to his knees to help her. They were surrounded in an instant by a crowd of people aching to assist. The lady rose shakily to her feet, smiling her thanks. The old man put his arm around her and ushered her into the warmth of a nearby café.

He was lonely.

The thought almost blindsided him. He, Max Grayland, who'd carefully built his life so he needed no one, was lonely.

How could he be lonely? He had this new person in his life, a beautiful little girl he'd grown to love. Back home he had Eliza, and Karen and her little Harry, increasingly belonging, increasingly filling the apartment with charm and laughter.

At work there were people everywhere.

He was surrounded, so how could he be lonely?

They'd been walking past shop windows full of brightly lit Christmas tableaux. Phoebe had been fascinated but was now drifting to contented sleep. He needed to get her home. And there was another jolt. *Home.*

How come, filled with all these people, his apartment didn't feel like home?

It must be Christmas, he decided savagely. He hated this time of year. It did his head in. And this year, once again he couldn't hide away with his accounts and a formal dinner with his friends.

Karen and Eliza would both be spending the day with their families.

It'd be just him and Phoebe.

Oh, for heaven's sake. He was getting maudlin. What was different? He could still bring in his accounts and work when Phoebe slept. And when she was awake…they could have fun.

They'd have more fun if Sunny was here.

His phone pinged in his jacket pocket and he almost lunged to reach it. He'd set his emails to silent. They were a huge constant in his life, almost overwhelming, but there was one email address he'd given priority to, and set up an alert.

Sunny.

And the words on the screen were heart-wrenching.

Hi Max

Sorry for the silence. I had to make a decision whether to tell you and decided not to. We didn't want you making some heroic effort to come for something that really affected only our family. But I need to let you know now.

Pa died a week ago last Sunday, suddenly, in his sleep, from a massive stroke. He'd had a lovely afternoon in the garden you've helped make so beautiful. All of us had been here for one of Gran's roasts, which he presided over. He didn't eat much but he seemed happy and contented as Gran and I helped him to bed. He made one of his awful puns that made us giggle, then hugged us goodnight and went to sleep. And didn't wake.

So his passing was as good as it could be. That doesn't mean we're not all gutted, but we know to count our blessings.

We had his funeral in the little church you came to with us, the church he and Gran have attended all their lives. It was lovely. Now it's hard to believe it's over but we're trying to pick up the pieces. All our care has to be for Gran. She'd been needed so much for so long and suddenly she's lost. We're caring for her as best we can but her grief...

I don't know how to help her and it's doing my head in.

Enough, though. You don't need to worry, we'll get through this.

Your hamper arrived yesterday. It has pride

of place under the Christmas tree but we're not opening it until Christmas morning. Though I'll admit I had a peek and saw the cherry liqueurs. Thank you. That's one thing I can now remember that I can forget.

We hope you and Phoebe have a lovely Christmas Day. I suspect all the kids will text you after they open the hamper, but I thought I should give you this heads-up first.

Christmas will be strange but it'll still happen.
Love you
Sunny

He didn't move. He couldn't. Shoppers, Christmas trees, bundles of gifts on legs, had to detour around the man standing in the middle of the pavement staring at his phone.

John was dead and he hadn't known.

Sunny would be gutted.

But more… His thoughts didn't stay with Sunny. They moved tangentially to Ruby, to the lovely old lady who'd taken in her five grandchildren and loved them so fiercely. And to the rest of Sunny's family. He imagined them at the funeral, young men and women fiercely protecting their gran. Gutted with grief. Loving…

He should have been there.

Home.

Why did the word slam back and stay? Why was it so powerful it didn't let him move?

He crouched down, almost involuntarily, and gathered Phoebe up into his arms. She was almost asleep, but happy to be hugged. She nuzzled into his neck, warm and secure.

Loved.

Sunny had given him this.

Home.

The tableau in the store behind him changed its tune from a corny rendition of *Jingle Bells* to a softer, lovelier melody.

Silent Night.

Sleep in heavenly peace...

That was what Phoebe was doing, he thought as her warm little body curved into his. Sleeping in peace.

Knowing she was loved.

And across the world... Sunny would be sleeping alone because he, Max Grayland, thought independence was everything.

He thought again of that front row pew at the funeral. Of grief. Loss went with love, he thought. That was why he'd held himself so tight, so rigid, so aloof. To deny himself something he wanted to be a part of so much it was a physical pain.

Sunny...

He was walking. He was moving automatically back towards the apartment, pushing the stroller with one hand, cradling Phoebe with the other, because there was no way he was putting her down.

He needed her.

And there was another flash of insight so great it almost blindsided him. He'd taken on Phoebe's care because she needed him but now...

He needed her.

He could never go back to what he had been. His defences had been breached and he didn't want them.

And his feet kept moving. He knew what he wanted and he was a man on his way to get it.

He had four days before Christmas. No. Three days, he reminded himself because Australia was almost a day ahead.

There was so much to organise...but if there was one thing Max Grayland was good at it was organising.

There was so much to hope for...and that was one thing he wasn't good at. Max Grayland liked certainty. He liked his world being ordered. He liked...

No. He didn't like any more, he reminded himself. He loved and that was a whole new ball game.

It meant that life as he knew it was about to turn upside down.

CHAPTER THIRTEEN

IT WAS PUTTING one foot in front of the other. Going through the motions. Getting through it.

They'd discussed—briefly—going out for Christmas dinner. Taking a picnic to the park. Booking into a restaurant. Anything to take the focus off the empty chair, the empty space, the emptiness of grief. But in the end Gran needed the quietness of this place, time with her family. So the kids were all here.

Sam was manfully carving the roast, trying to pretend it was no big deal to be doing what Pa had done for years. Gran was pretending to eat. They were pretending to laugh at the dumb jokes in the bonbons. They were wearing silly party hats, thinking of stories to fill the silence. Anything...

Sunny was trying not to watch Gran. She was trying not to cry.

And there was a part of her that was trying not to think of last Christmas. Trying not to wonder what Max was doing. Trying not to think of Max and Phoebe sharing Christmas on the other side of the world.

I could have made it better for them, a little voice kept saying in the back of her head, but she only had to look at Gran to know she was right to be here.

'What goes ninety-nine thump, ninety-nine thump, ninety-nine thump?' Daisy demanded, her grin as natural as she could make it.

And they answered in chorus, 'A centipede with a wooden leg.' They'd heard this joke for years and suddenly…it made things better. A little. That they could shout the answer, that they'd shared this joke for so many Christmases.

That they were family.

Except Max wasn't here.

He wasn't family, Sunny told herself fiercely. He wasn't.

And then the doorbell rang.

'It's the timer for the pudding,' Daisy said—how could it be anything else but the cooking timer?—and Sunny's heart rate settled. It had lurched…

But then… No. She knew the sound of the timer.

She knew the sound of the doorbell.

And so did Gran. She half rose and Tom glanced at her and then at Sunny and headed for the door.

And Sunny tried hard to stay where she was. It was a crazy thought—what she'd just thought. It couldn't be.

But…

'It's Phoebe!' Tom's shout echoed through the house, from top to bottom. 'Hey, it's Phoebe and she's *growed*! Wow, she's growed! Phoebe, what have they been feeding you? Hey, gorgeous, come to Uncle Tom. And Max. Is that you under that baby stuff? Come on out. Come on in.'

And Sunny's heart forgot to race.

Sunny's heart almost stopped altogether.

There was nothing like a baby to cheer Christmas. Gran hugged Phoebe like a lifeline. Phoebe cooed and chuckled and banged a spoon on whatever Gran was eating. Gran ended up covered with soggy pudding and totally distracted and... almost happy.

Time out from grief...

'Thank you for the chocolates, young man,' she told Max. 'They're almost as good as the ones Sunny used to buy.'

The family hooted with laughter, and Sunny grinned and tried not to feel...as if she had no idea how she was feeling.

Max ate as if he hadn't eaten for a year. The kids told him the joke about the centipede and couldn't believe he'd never heard it. He talked and laughed as if he belonged.

And Sunny tried to eat, tried not to gaze at him, tried to smile, tried to figure how to get her thoughts back into some sort of order.

'I had to come,' Max had said simply as he'd arrived. He'd hugged Gran and then he'd walked around the table to where Sunny sat, feeling frozen. He'd touched her hair, a feather touch, that was all, and then he'd sat where Sam had set a fast place. But that touch…

With dinner done, the house settled for the afternoon. Phoebe napped in a makeshift cot upstairs next to Gran's bed because that was where Gran wanted her. Gran slept too, probably the first peaceful sleep she'd fallen into since Pa had died. The dishes were done. Christmas afternoon stretched as it always did, sated, sleepy, as if Christmas was over, but this time, for Sunny, it felt…it was as if the gifts hadn't been opened yet?

'So…basketball?' Tom demanded but Max shook his head.

'I need to talk to Sunny.'

And the way he said it…

The look on the kids' combined faces was priceless. They fell over themselves to gear up and get out to the hoops without looking at their sister.

They disappeared as Sunny and Max walked out of the front door, through the now beautifully kept front garden and along the lanes they'd walked twelve months ago today.

Why was he here? So much had changed, Sunny thought, yet so much stayed the same.

Her life was here, she reminded herself. If possible, she was needed even more.

'I've missed you,' Max said, and her heart seemed to clench. She couldn't handle more pressure. She loved this man. She also loved the little girl currently sleeping beside Gran but it couldn't be allowed to matter.

Her place was here.

No. Not here. Not right here. She was walking beside Max, and she thought that this was where she didn't need to be.

Oh, but she wanted…

'I haven't come to put more pressure on you,' he said. They were walking side by side, close but not as close as lovers. Close enough for friends?

That was what they were, she reminded herself. Friends who emailed once a week. Friends who'd almost been something more.

He was still talking, softly, almost to himself. 'I'd like to say I don't need you,' he said into the stillness. Their feet seemed to be walking automatically. He wasn't looking at her but at the path ahead, as if what he was saying wasn't monumentally important. 'I'd like to say everything I'm about to offer you is for you, Sunny, and has nothing to do with me. I'd like to be that selfless but I can't do it.'

'I don't… I don't understand.'

He paused then and took her hand, twisting her to face him. 'Sunny… Let me say what I've been thinking. And I've been thinking…what I offered you back in Manhattan was monumentally selfish. It was all about me. It was an offer that gave me a wife, a lover, a mother for Phoebe, a partner I could admire and love for the rest of my life.

But it was all on my terms. You left and I tried to understand, but I couldn't get it. I didn't see how I could change my life for a life on your terms.'

'But…'

'No, let me finish. Sunny, three days ago I was standing in a Manhattan street watching families prepare for Christmas and your email came through. John was dead. And I stood there like I was frozen and all I could think of was that I wanted to be in that front pew at your grandfather's funeral. I wanted to be with you. But it was more than that. It was huge. I wanted to have the right to hug your gran, to hug the kids. I know this sounds dumb, maybe still even selfish, but I wanted to have the right to grieve like you were all grieving.'

He hesitated then, as if he was waiting for her to comment but she couldn't say a word. The whole world seemed to be holding its breath. Waiting for…what?

The warmth of the day was eased by the shade of the massive gum trees overhead. There were bird calls, muted but lovely, and the smell of eucalypt was everywhere. These were the sounds and smell of an Australian Christmas—but right now who was thinking of Christmas?

'Do you know what I finally figured?' Max asked at last. 'I wanted the right to be gutted.'

She stared at him, confused. 'Okay,' she confessed. 'I don't get it.'

'So I'll try and explain.' He took both her hands in his. His gaze met hers and held and her heart twisted before he even began to speak. Or maybe it didn't twist. Maybe it simply stilled. Hoped…

'Sunny, I'm the son of parents who never gave a toss,' he told her. 'I was important only because I was the heir. I was raised by a succession of nannies but even they were impermanent because I was moving all the time. My parents moved from one country to another, from one partner to another, and I was simply the kid who had to be fitted in with whoever's life I didn't complicate too much at the time. And whenever I started to love a nanny, or be fond of a step-parent, or love a puppy given to me on a whim…there was a Christmas gift that broke my heart…well, life simply moved on and what I loved was left behind.'

'Oh, Max…'

'Yeah, tough,' he said and managed a lopsided smile. 'It was nowhere near as tough as you had it, Sunny, but you know what? I came out of my childhood with an armour so thick I thought it couldn't be pierced. You, though, you never did armour. You never could. You love and you love and that's your thing. That's who you are, Sunny. And me…it's taken a woman like you to pierce the armour I've built. You showed me almost instantly the kind of life Phoebe would have if I didn't love her. I've learned—sort of—but it's taken me a year to realise…if I'm learning to fight to keep

Phoebe from that kind of isolation, maybe... I should fight for me too.'

'But...how?' The world had stilled. The world held its breath.

'By learning to be family?' His words were tentative. 'I've adopted Phoebe now—did you know? She now shares part of your name. Phoebe Raye Grayland. I called her that because you seem part of us, but...we need more.'

'We...we had this conversation back in Manhattan.'

'Yeah, but then I didn't get it.' He dropped her hands and drew her in by the waist so she was curved against him. 'Back then I thought...you and me and Phoebe would be enough. And I could do it part-time. I could pay people to fill the gaps. So that's what I tried. Even this Christmas when I did my Christmas planning I decided I could play with Phoebe in the morning and work on business imperatives—get back to my real life—while she slept. And then your email arrived and suddenly my life seemed...the wrong way up. And I thought...where is my real life? It's not in the gaps of time where Phoebe sleeps. It's not even in Manhattan. Sunny, I need it to be with you.'

'But it won't work.' She was close to tears, immeasurably distressed. It'd be so easy to sink into this man's arms, to say yes, to love him for ever. But the thought of that huge, designer furnished apartment in Manhattan, the thought of staff to care for Phoebe so the baby wouldn't interfere with their lives, the thought of Max being gone six days out of seven, and on the end of his phone the rest of the time—it was like a cold, blank wall. She'd seen how much of an effort it had cost him to step away for those weeks. She'd heard the promises he'd made to callers...

I'll be back on deck at the end of the month. Let's keep everything on hold...'

'Your life's on hold now?' she asked, forcing herself to ask, knowing it had to be said. 'You've taken time off to come over and ask me again?'

'You think this is the same?' His hold on her tightened as if he was fearful she might disappear. 'Sunny, I've had an epiphany.'

'That sounds...painful?'

He grinned but his smile was uncertain. 'It was,' he told her. 'I had it when your email came through, right there on the streets of Manhattan, and it almost knocked me sideways. I was bumped by about six Christmas trees while I was coming to terms with it. And maybe those trees bumped some sense into my thick head. Sunny, what if we make it all about you? What if...instead of asking you to be part of my life, if I ask to be part of your life?'

She was struggling here. Really struggling. *Keep it light*, she told herself desperately. *Do not allow yourself to hope...*

'What? Share my mop?' she managed. 'I'm not sure the hotel approves of job-sharing.'

'Are you so attached to your mop you wouldn't hand it in if a better offer came your way?'

'It's…it's a very good mop.' This was dumb but it was all she could come up with. 'It's industrial strength with a nice blue handle.'

'I've seen it.'

'No, you haven't. My job's been upgraded. I only mop in an emergency now and they've issued me a new one. Didn't you even notice my last mop was ancient?'

'No.' His smile was tender. 'How could I? I was too busy noticing you.'

'Compliments won't get you mop sharing.' This was ridiculous, but that was how this conversation felt. Ridiculous.

But Max's words didn't sound ridiculous at all.

'Okay, here's the thing,' he told her tenderly, lovingly. 'Three days ago I stood on a Manhattan street and watched families. All sorts of families. Friends, kids, grandparents, lovers. I watched love of all sorts, people getting ready for Christmas. Messy Christmases. Christmases in all sorts of circumstances. And even though I'd just adopted Phoebe it didn't seem the same. But I stood there and thought of you as a kid making sock puppets for your family. I thought of you fighting for your siblings, putting them first. When I proposed eleven months ago that's what I thought I was buying. I wanted that kind of commitment, Sunny. I wanted it for me and for Phoebe. But what I didn't see until now was that…it has to come from me. I got it wrong. Sunny, I want to be allowed to fight for you. More… I want to be allowed to need you, as the kids, as your gran needs you. But I want the rest too. I want you to need me. I love you, Sunny, and I need us to be a family. I want to be a part of your family, and I'll do…whatever it takes.'

'You…you already…you've said…'

'That I'll send you to university. That I'll pay for nannies, housekeepers. That I'll pay for your family here to be looked after. Yes, I said all that, and you know what? It cost me nothing. Because there was no me in the equation. Sunny, now I'm asking you to marry me, and in return…whatever you want…'

'I don't have a price.' It was a snap; frustration, fear, everything she had was in that word. Did he not get it?

'I'm not talking price,' he said, evenly now as if he finally understood what she was saying. 'I'm talking me. My commitment to your life. My love. Sunny, how would you feel if I moved here? If we did this big old house up so it'll last another hundred years…?'

'It's not ours,' she whispered, trying fiercely to be practical. 'It's a life tenancy until Gran dies.'

'Then we find the person who eventually in-

herits and make them an offer they can't refuse—
we can do that.'

'You can't move here. Your life's in Manhattan.'

'My apartment's in Manhattan. My life's all
over the world. Do you know how much time I
spend in the air? But that can stop. It will stop.'

'It's what you are.'

'It's what I've been raised to be. It's not what I
want to be for the rest of my life. My company's
full of extraordinary talent. With my father gone, I
can run things the way I want. I can control things
here as well as in Manhattan. And I hear there
are very good architecture courses in Australia.'

'Max, I don't want a nanny!'

'You won't need one. Phoebe's not your responsibility. She's mine.'

'But I love her.' The words were out before she
could stop them and Max's expression changed.

'Of course you do. That's your specialty and
that's pretty much what I expected you to say.
Which is part of what I've figured. That loving me
shouldn't mean loving anyone else any less. Take
me as an example if you like. Twelve months ago I
didn't love anyone. Now… I love Phoebe. The pain
when I knew Pa was dead was like a kick in the
guts. I care for your Gran and for Daisy and Sam
and Chloe and Tom. And there's more. Twelve
months ago I hardly knew my housekeeper and
now…not only do I know about every one of her
grandchildren, she even carted me out so Phoebe

and I could help her choose gifts. And Karen, our nanny… She and her little boy… They've learned to love Phoebe and in turn they've twisted their way into my heart too. I think…if you do agree to my proposal…that I'll leave them in my apartment in caretaker mode. With Eliza, too. Karen dreams of being a potter. With Eliza's help to care for Harry, she could do that.'

'You'd let…you'd have them stay in that apartment…?'

'It'd still be there, then,' he said. 'A base when we…if we wanted to visit New York. Because there might be times…'

'Max…'

'Because I would be busy,' he said, with the air of someone putting all their cards on the table and the consequences would have to play out. 'Sunny, I can't let go of the corporation. It's too big, too important; it has the power to affect too many lives.'

'And you care about it.' Her vision was starting to blur. She never wept but her cheeks were wet now. 'You want it to make a difference.'

'I do,' he admitted. 'Dad did so much damage but he's left me in a position where not only can I right the damage, I can move the company forward to do great things. But…' He took a deep breath. 'Sunny, I used to think I could do it on my own but I can't. I know that now. Sure, I can do a little, but with you beside me, with my family around me, with love… Sunny, we could conquer the world.'

'The world…'

'Why not? But you… When it comes to the world or you… Sunny, you'll always come first. You always will. So how about it, my love? Will you trust me enough to put your hand in mine? To take me on? To haul me back when I get out of line, when I stop remembering what's important?'

And then he paused and the pause stretched out. He was looking down into her eyes and she was trying her hardest to meet his gaze but tears were tracking down her face. She couldn't stop them. She needed a tissue but her hands were in his and there was no way she was letting go.

And then he kissed her, gently, on each cheek, kissing away her tears.

'Sunny,' he said gently, softly, lovingly. 'Will you teach me to love? Will you let me into your heart?'

And there was only one answer. Of course there was.

Together they could take on the world?

There was no need for that, she thought mistily. Who needed the world?

Max was here. Max loved her.

'You're already there,' she whispered back. 'Oh, Max…oh, my love, you can share my mop any time you want.'

Was Christmas the time for a wedding?

Yes, it was. It hadn't seemed right to hold it straight after they'd lost Pa. It had seemed somehow fitting that they waited for a full year. In truth they might have waited longer—they were so close, so truly family there seemed little need for a formal wedding and Gran's grief needed time to play out. But finally Gran decided to shed her grief enough to move on. On a warm spring day, while Sunny and Max were helping Phoebe plant strawberries—with mixed results—she came to find them.

Fixing Max with a gimlet eye, she made her demand. 'Well, young man. When are you going to make an honest woman out of my granddaughter?'

'Sunny's been wearing my engagement ring for ten months,' Max said, grinning and tugging Sunny to stand beside him. 'She's had my heart for much longer. I believe we're waiting for you to say the word.'

'Because?'

'Because we want you to be happy at our wedding,' Max said simply. 'Sunny won't have it any other way, and neither will I. If you feel you can cope with a celebration…'

'I knew it.' Ruby smiled mistily at both of them 'I was just lying down on my bed thinking bridal and I thought… I bet they're waiting for me. And then I thought Pa would have my hide if I don't say something. So how about Christmas Eve? All the kids will be home. What a truly splendid time that'd be.'

So here he was, in the little church he'd first

attended two days after he'd met Sunny. He'd expected this to be a small affair but Gran was having none of it and she'd bulldozed Sunny and Max along with her.

'All your friends from the hotel, Sunny—I know you haven't worked there for almost a year but they were nice to you. And Max, your friends from New York and those nice ladies who look after your apartment...'

'It's too far to expect anyone to come,' Max told her. 'And Karen and Eliza can't...' And then he stopped because he thought... Why not use a fraction of what his company earned to bring Eliza and Karen and Harry, Karen's little son, here? They'd been part of the first year of Phoebe's life and somehow they were no longer employees. They were friends.

On this day there were so many people here that he once would have called acquaintances but with Sunny by his side he somehow now called friends.

And Max was aware of them, and glad of them, but right now, as the music soared to announce the arrival of his bride, he had no room for anything but Sunny.

First came the ring-bearers, two tots, Karen's four-year-old Harry leading two-year-old Phoebe, both intent, serious, knowing the importance of the job in hand. Or Harry did. Phoebe simply thought that if Harry was carrying a cushion with a ring, then she would too.

Then came the bridesmaids, Daisy and Chloe, because how could they not be bridesmaids? Sam and Tom were standing beside him as groomsmen, because that seemed right too.

Then came Ruby, dressed in royal purple. The maids wore pink, but: 'Purple's such a stately colour and if I can't feel stately today I never can,' Ruby had decreed. She was matron of honour, for how could she be anything else?

'You don't want to give me away?' Sunny had asked and Ruby had chuckled.

'My love, you've stood on your own two feet since the day you were born. You're giving your heart and you're taking one in return and you can do that all on your own.'

And she surely could.

And now she was at the doorway, starting her walk down the aisle towards him.

Max thought briefly of the great churches of Manhattan, of the world. He thought briefly of the photographs of his parents' wedding, a society wedding like no other.

This was right though. This was...real.

Outside, a cacophony of grass parrots was competing with Handel for sound honours. The church was surrounded by a sea of bcrimson bottlebrush. It was Christmas but more. The whole country seemed festive, as if this was truly something to celebrate.

And it was. For Sunny was walking towards

him, ethereal in her loveliness. Her gown had been her grandmother's, cream silk with a high mandarin collar, tiny pearl buttons, a tight fitted bodice and a skirt that seemed to almost float. She'd left her curls hanging free but her sisters had threaded tiny rosebuds through. She trod steadily down the aisle, purposeful as ever, and he thought he'd never seen anyone so lovely.

He couldn't take his eyes from her. She smiled and smiled and as she reached him, as her gaze met his, as her hand slid into his palm, he felt as if he'd been granted the world.

'Want to see my bouquet?' she whispered and it brought him up with a jolt. *What?*

He hauled his eyes from hers to the flowers she was carrying, a magnificent arrangement of crimson bottlebrush, white gypsophila—baby's breath—and four perfect frangipani...

And tucked inside was a tiny bottle, label up. *Stain remover?*

'I figure I met you trying to remove a stain,' she whispered, smiling and smiling. 'And I didn't succeed on one spot, but you know what? We've cleaned up so much more. Loneliness, distrust, distance... So I thought...maybe we should go into this prepared. Stain remover out front. Just in case.'

And he grinned. His gorgeous, wonderful Sunny. It was a wonder she wasn't carrying her mop.

'Great idea,' he whispered. 'But I can't see the

need. I pretty much see our future as stain-free.
You want to give the vicar a say and get ourselves
married? Put our trust in love?'

'Yes,' she said and beamed and, even though it
was out of order to do it right then, she stood on
tiptoes and kissed him. 'Yes, I do, Max Grayland.
You and me and stain remover… We can take on
the world.'

'Let's start with each other.'

'Let's,' she said and he kissed her back.

The music ceased. Even the parrots in the trees
outside seemed to hush.

Christmas…the time of miracles.

Maybe this was a small miracle in the scheme
of things but right now it felt huge. It was huge.

It was one marriage between two people who
truly loved so, without further ado, Sunny Raye
and Max Grayland turned together to become one.

* * * * *

If you enjoyed this story, check out these other great reads from Marion Lennox

REUNITED WITH HER SURGEON PRINCE
STRANDED WITH THE SECRET
BILLIONAIRE
FALLING FOR HER WOUNDED HERO
STEPPING INTO THE PRINCE'S WORLD

All available now!